CW00751295

An Afterclap of Fate

Mallory on Everest

An Afterclap of Fate

Mallory on Everest

by

Charles Lind

Published by The Ernest Press

Reprinted 2006

ISBN 0 948153 84 9

Typeset by Stanningley Serif
Printed by St Edmundsbury Press, Bury St Edmunds IP33 3TZ

Contents

I

Because it was there . . . as if waiting for the coming of the perfect knight, a monster, lord of all: the anvil of the elements.

I had to step off the map, into *terra incognita,* to find the East Rongbuk Glacier, which led us through a maze of melt channels, full of 'wrinkles and frostic furrowes', into a Wonderland World of towering, jagged pinnacles of ice.

A forest of glistening spires gleaming above opalescent frozen-pools: a primordial ice-world that during the day became a burning, sun-reflecting furnace. And we had to march in through it, in order to reach the foot of the North Col, which held the promise of the prospect of a first ascent; the goal my heart was set upon.

Everest is a massive giant, an awesome triumph of chthonic forces, that rises up and up to unfurl its sovereign snow-plume icily in the sky; a crystallomancy for the wind.

The absolute scale of the vision had me almost beaten for words. A tougher job than I had bargained for. The summit pyramid of its great, spire peak, gnawed all the way up by high altitude winds, to the place where desire ends . . . twenty nine thousand and two feet up in the thin, frigid air.

I feared from the start the immense, vertiginous hold . . . the awesome sense of purpose its inhuman challenge gave my life, the hidden crevasse of self-doubt. Amongst my fellow climbers it was said, that I was the greatest in unfulfilled achievement.

Now the spectacle of undying fame, an overwhelming height of immortality towered fantastically above the clouds. The opportunity of a lifetime . . . the chance to forge such a name.

'The result is nothing, dear Galahad', wrote my friend and mentor Geoffrey Winthrop Young, 'compared to the rightness of the attempt . . . Good fortune! And the resolution to return . . . even in the face of ambition'

II

From long observation of the contours, a sense of the physiognomy of the mountain, something of its character begins to emerge. I understand the truth now of Ruskin's observation, that no architecture is so haughty as that which is simple.

I took a photograph of it in '21, from Ri-ring, that I thought almost did it justice . . . the photographic plate had written on it 'Fine Grain Slow'. And in fine grain and slowly, that's how you need to picture it . . . a monumental, intimidating colossus . . . an awesome phenomenon of the Earth . . . a pinnacle of geological gigantism . . . the crescendo of the sublime.

And always our most implacable enemy . . . the north-west wind. The north-west wind is the storm breath of the monsoon, harrying its crystal-seeded clouds to rupture here into deathly white-out days of icy, driven snow.

It is a desert region at this altitude, an azoic world, undisturbed by even the most primitive, ruderal life. Only the sun and wind disturb the stasis.

The elemental, restless hymn of the wind . . .

When it is quiet, you can occasionally hear the graunching sounds, echoing up from the great, white glaciers: the slow, grinding tides of perennial ice.

Imagine stepping through the Door of the Coincidence of Opposites, into an Alice in Wonderland world, where it is possible to be sunburnt and to get frostbite at the same time.

As the atmospheric pressure drops, the higher up you go, so your heart must increase the rate of its beat to cope. The paucity of oxygen in the atmosphere also makes breathing a conscious act of will. The air itself is cold, dry and thin, with a faint, slight headiness of death.

At this height the sheer limpidity of the light, and the spellbind of the poignant sense of the fragile miracle of life . . .

I love snow, and all the forms of the radiant Frost . . .

Out of the perfect symmetry of the raindrop crystallises the hexagonal symmetry of the snowflake, therein lies the Ariadnean clue to all creation . . . the crystallising out of an initial, perfect symmetry.

Thou hast a voice great Mountain, to repeal
Large codes of fraud and woe; not understood
By all, but which the wise, and great and good
Interpret, or make felt, or deeply feel.

It's all too easy to become ensnared in an increasingly narrow and unreflective mind . . . and end one's days as Merlin, enchanted into the confines of a cave. The mountain has always been seen as a symbol of spiritual transcendence, the allegorical seat of divine natures . . . and its ascension a metaphor for the process of inner realisation.

Old General Bruce told the High Lama we came as pilgrims, members of a mountain worshipping sect. Lama Chongraysay warned us, in his reply, that the deity of the place was a very terrible one.

III

Only a few days ago with Geoffrey Bruce, the General's young nephew, the whole show bloody crashed. Our gasless attempt on the summit fizzled out . . . a wretched affair, the 'Tigers', our strongest porters, succumbing finally to the wind, losing all heart and stamina in that region of laborious breath.

And poor Geoffrey's heart was dilated, as a result of the appallingly tremendous strain, by two and a half ribs. An alarming epitonic condition. But my own heart simply wasn't in it . . . I knew that an epic of effort was insufficient . . . we simply hadn't enough puff to see us there.

Neither had Norton and Somervell, on their following whack at it . . . 'where Mallory blows', the boffins said, 'what chance is there for others'.

But where Mallory blows and blows . . . reduced to the halt and desperate agony of a heaving pair of lungs, near drowning for want of oxygen, what hope is there even for Mallory.

So now I'm back with the oxygen apparatus and Sandy, the way I'd planned it from the start.

IV

A heavenly reach above the yak-dung line, it's a bed-sock altitude Camp VI. The frugal Hotel Mount Everest, not like the silver service one in Darjeeling, but our light, two-man, Alpine Meade tent, huddled in a cleft in the North ridge, its canvas constantly fretting in the wind, precariously perched on a platform of rocks. You can't beat a bed of weathered rock for a good night's sleep at 26,000ft. The effort to overcome the nausea and eat.

I look down on a vast, mountainous world, the ruck and rout of riotous witnesses to a convocation of the primordial forces, awesome testimony of the elemental powers.

Above me soars Everest's plumed peak, its icy crest high in the rare, breath-taxing air . . . Hope's bright vision vouchsafed and cloudless now . . . 'clear cut in azure'.

I couldn't keep my eyes off the summit. The great, white pyramid vaulted in the ethereal reaches of the sky. It looked now so tantalisingly close, the siren draw of its dominating presence. I was sure the North-east Ridge would 'go'.

This afternoon I prospected the route, going lightly on one cylinder of oxygen, in almost perfect weather for climbing. Up towards the first rock step, to gain a better view of the summit. I needed to get a clearer sense of just how far it was to the top . . . or as we used to say in the Gunners . . . the range to the target. Trying to judge the critical equation of distance over time . . . a quiet hour of decision alone with the mountain.

Mountaineering is as much a test of temper and temperament as it is of physique . . . and as I turn back now, the view below is all of Delectable Mountains in sunshine, as if in beaming affirmation of my resolve.

But it's so far been much harder than in '22, the crevasse and the ice chimney obstructing the North Col, the wind and weather conditions being far more severe. The wind is the real killer. And if our summit attempt is to succeed, we depend upon the mountain being kind. Good weather and the fizz of 'English air' to get us through the final gates of altitude.

The sunlight, the prospect of a fine day tomorrow, and the inspiratory aid of the oxygen, all serve to inspire me with renewed hope, and the feeling that our luck has changed. I returned to the tent with a quiet confidence, I had never felt so good on Everest before.

Sandy came up to greet me with a flask of soup, no ministering angel was ever more welcome. Tomorrow would be our day . . . and what a course.

Tonight the sunset was beyond everything, more wonderful than the one I saw from the Nesthorn in 1909. The stupendous scale of mountainscape, I watched as the East Rongbuk Glacier drowned in shadow, until it became an arm of gathering darkness, surrounded by a world of sun-blushed peaks, as the Alpenglow caught fire on ice and snow.

A transmuted world of gold and delicate pinks, whole summits emblazoned into subtle yellows, the profoundly mysterious alchemy of the light; until finally Everest alone held a glowing corona in the dark. I felt the temperature drop in my bones.

Sandy was tinkering with the oxygen sets, checking fragile rubber tubing, and gently adjusting torque on nuts and bolts. He had such a feel for mechanical things . . . it was like watching a musician tuning up.

I tried to recite Gray's *Elegy* from memory and was baffled to find that I no longer had it by heart. I ended up trying not to think how, in our age, the paths of glory can depend so horrendously on fragile valves and the torsion of a nut . . . as if the strain on one's heart were not enough.

And all the world a solemn stillness holds . . .

Save for our heavy, laboured breathing, the painful sound of two asthmatics. I always feel my best on the eve of the fray.

Sandy started explaining, for the umpteenth time, about the threads used on the oxygen apparatus. Siebe Gorman had specified Standard Whitworth, he had duly brought a set of taps and dies to suit . . . only to discover that the buggers had used B.A. threads. Well, if that wasn't the B-all to end all, damn it! All his efforts had been bloody nearly scuppered.

I realised it was time to change the subject, if only for peace of mind and sanity's sake, he would be telling me about Swedish, Vibrax steel again next, and a little mechanical engineering goes a long way.

"Have a biscuit, old chap. They're my favourite, Ginger Nuts"

"Tomorrow we'll be on the summit", I said. "And the next day we'll get down to

Camp III. A triumphant welcome, applause and cheers for two such remarkably splendid fellows."

"God, the hell-freezing, glacial cold of Camp III . . . that perishing, bitter moraine. One final, trial by ordeal then . . . the desperate 'double mark time' on a flat stone to try and drive out the terrible bone-piercing, flesh-biting cold, before turning in for an attempt to sleep, with the deadening cold seeping back into our bodies like an invisible incoming tide. With luck it should be our last bloody night, in ruddy 'Balmoral' or sodding 'Sandringham'."

"We'll send the signal down to Norton to dispatch the coded telegram to *The Times* . . . so the 'Thunderer' can break the great news. Then down again the following day to Camp II. We'll be gloriously lazy and take the 'Avalanche Route', to the culinary genius of Karmi and the 'Roarer Cooker', the honoured guests of old Shebbeare . . . Your friend, the 'King of Camp II', will treat us lavishly . . . as it behoves a king to do . . . even if he does look and smell more like a Piltdown man."

"And if we get caught by the monsoon, just think, we'll savour, once again, the gastronomic delights of Karmi Cha . . . that nightmare haunting cha. The inimitable, surreal brew of beans and tea, with that piquant admixture of kerosene oil; the bastard creation of desperate circumstances, for which all poor blighters are truly, damn grateful."

"Nostalgia for Karmi Cha . . . it must be the altitude."

"But where was I . . . ah, yes, just reaching the finale. And so then finally, at last, the long slog back down the weary '*Via Dolorosa*' to Base Camp. The heroes of the hour return hip-hip hoorah! A goose-pimpling X-bath in lukewarm water, clean clothes and restored to pukka sahibdom, smelling of Dr. Parke Davis's germicidal soap . . . we'll be all ready for the Champagne Dinner."

"By the warm light of the clockwork paraffin lamps, the Montebello 1915 . . . Quails truffled in Foie Gras, and not forgetting plenty of Harris's sausages."

"We'll be fêted, endlessly congratulated, all that ballyhoo and slapping on the back. We'll be the toast of the Whymper Tents."

"To the two Birkenhead men of the party", I said holding up my tin of Ideal milk, with a suitably exaggerated bravura. "We'll be front page on the *Birkenhead News!*"

Sandy, his blue eyes lambent, was just aburst with laughter. The tent exploded lightly . . . the effervescent sound of happiness.

And now, through the open canvas flap of the tent, the ancient scintillation of the stars, that bright cantillation of the light, seemed almost a whisper closer.

It will be a great adventure . . .

V

There's something about this hour . . . charged with the coming of dawn . . . a primeval echo of the sacrament of genesis . . . the primordial sense of its hallowedness . . . the atavistic shiver in the soul.

And through the tent flap now, I can clearly see a bright quiver of stars. Stars before dawn, with that hard crystalline look of jewels, are a good sign. We should have the weather on our side.

The beacon herald of coming day, the snow capped, summit of Everest above us, etched in a pale, silver light. Down here, all is enshadowed in the dark, still frost-fast in the freezing cold. Day is dawning auspiciously . . . mercifully, a none too breezy call.

And kindled now in sunlight, the snowy peaks of Cho Oyu and Gyachung Kang, flame out against the ebbing tide of night. The gods, it seems, have smiled.

We've had a restful night, thanks to oxygen and Sandy's skill in improvising the set up. I owe this piece of canny good sense to George Finch, and I'm sure it has eased my wretched, hacking cough. And it's made a very noticeable, visible difference, our hands and faces are not discoloured that deathly blue, symptomatic of cyanosis. So we don't have hands like the Jumblies . . . even if we are in a horribly 'Torrible Zone'.

Recalling the minor disaster in '22, with the frozen tin of Heinz spaghetti, I remembered to cosset a tin of food inside my sleeping bag, to keep it coddled and unfrozen. It's on such absurdly little things as this, that success can now depend.

I had wanted to be off early, to make a moonlight start . . . but the stupefying age it takes to do anything at this altitude. The all too necessary attempt at a hearty, pukka breakfast and the aeons it takes to prepare. Something choice to set us up, lukewarm macaroni and tepid coffee; the gastronomic ordeal before the struggle to put on frozen boots, with the curious mineral taste of melted snow persisting in one's mouth. Poor Sandy, his lips are so cracked; eating is painfully unpleasant for him.

Yesterday morning, at Camp V, in an awkward moments clumsiness, I knocked the blasted Unna cooker over, sending it off to wildly plunge, bouncing out a shrill death rattle, on a spectacularly busier career than its sputtering snow-melting. So I've been extremely careful this morning, ensuring the Unna cooker's safekeeping, by leaving it entirely in Sandy's charge. The wise delegation of responsibility . . . that hallmark of the experienced leader.

We're now almost ready, at last, the final checking of our pocket tiffin: Mintcake, Butter Scotch, prunes, raisins, chocolate and pemmican; and most vitally, our precious flasks.

I'll leave the electric torch, my candle-lantern is lighter . . . keep to the tried and tested, let Sandy do the pioneering.

The partnership of the young and the old, the new and traditional technologies; the *Light Blue* and the *Dark Blue* pulling together, Oxbridge for the summit.

Outside the tent, the first Fauve freaks of the Alpenglow . . . I'm stamping my feet to get the circulation going.

The last minute adjustments now to clothing . . . just getting the puttees right and tucking in the collar of my favourite, old silk shirt. Odd how you become so attached to these 'old friends', and so superstitious about them . . . the comforting charm of a luck-bringer.

God, how could so many layers feel so inadequate. As it is I feel as cumbered as a knight in armour. A modern knight in a fur-lined, motor cycle helmet . . . Sir Mallory enters the Lists . . . where's my bloody scarf?

This isn't just *Nanook of the North* . . . it's a Cherry-Garrard shiver of degrees below freezing . . . it fairly 'cruddles the blood' . . . I should have been an Emperor Penguin, all those lovely, insulating layers of subcutaneous fat.

And now, through my dragon-smoky breath, one of the planets shining above Changtse . . . a good auspice . . . all the omens are propitious. Zero hour . . . the day so looked forward to . . . and dreaded . . . this unearthly reality of the dream become real. Thank god for the bloody cold, galvanising one to get going.

Time now to pick up my oxygen: 'only rotters would use oxygen, so unsporting and un-British'. But I wisely had a change of heart, a grim lesson now painfully learnt, the wizard cross I've come to bear . . . the Irvine MK.V prototype.

The dead-weight load of the apparatus shouldered, heavy as a *memento mori:* my two silver bottles of salvation, cradled in their Bergen pack frame. Suitably attired now for an audience with the 'Grand Lunar' himself. Sound for the Sea of Tranquillity. All ready to discover the future. The cumbersome box of tricks waked now to provide the living air.

A body of England's breathing 'English air' . . .

Setting off to mount the 'gas offensive' . . . I can't hear if my armour is squeaking, although it's a bloody load for climbing.

But I'll leave Sandy to pioneer those new-fangled zip-pockets. Perhaps his machine-tooled zip will come into its own . . . someday on the moon. We could be the first men . . . the first men on top of the World.

We've the weather for it and if our luck holds out, the constant hiss of the oxygen, the life-giving hymn of the 'English air'.

'Look out for us crossing the rock band or going up the skyline at 8.00 a.m.'

That last tip for Noel, St. Noel of the Cameras, for his cinematograph, posterity and, dear god, the 'Glaxo-loving public'.

We've got to get up this time . . .

From the shade of his colourful, pink umbrella in '21, my companion, Guy Bullock, gave the odds as fifty-to-one. 'We'll give it our best whack . . . and do ourselves proud.'

My very own *bandobast* at last . . . using the boost of the gas, a rope of two, the original pairing. As Geoffrey said, personal relations are the secret of success . . . *esprit de pair* . . . the vital, mysterious chemistry. That and the practice of pace by sustained rhythm.

Posterity can only hope old Noel's got his clockwork camera purring. The Newman Sinclair with modifications suggested by the great Herbert Ponting.

Damn, the chilly shade of Scott looms . . . with all its crushing 'One Ton Dump' gloom. Let him rest in his heroic mould . . . time is ever an irreverent spirit. An impatient prodigal, the quintessence of the process of erosion, the sundering doom of the pomp of monuments . . . such is our remorseless wasting through the riddling of the years . . . we who are but for a time . . . so who dares dawdle.

No one with the amount of ground we've got to cover . . . and it's going to be some while yet, before Noel has us remotely in his finder telescope.

The adventures first, as the Griffin said.

VI

Yet once more, O ye Mountain, and once more
Ye Snow frigid with Icy, frosty hoar,
I reach toward your virgin Summit core,
Let not thy rude, inclement winds be too frore.

O, the exhilaration of it, so much more exciting than teaching worthy Milton, a heavy chore, to sappy youth in its pimple-blossom time; the prosaic memory of that now is such a bore.

And now my feet on crumping snow,
Set forth upon this splendid show . . .

How wholeheartedly I agree with Keats, 'the poetic character lives in gusto'. I would choose Blake's 'Energy is Eternal Delight' for my motto.

Looking for a line among the rocks now . . . thinking narrowly how a route might go . . . It's not just about having a good eye; you've got to have a feel for it as well, something instinctual in your bones. But it is a very unwise man who is not prepared to retrace his steps. Pride on occasion has to be swallowed. It's a stark truth to have to recognise . . . gut feelings sometimes can be wrong.

Still, as the now legendary Mummery, in his inimitable, droll style, has observed, mountains pass through three stages: from being an inaccessible peak, then to the most difficult climb there is, and finally, to be just an easy day for a lady. One might call it Mummery's Law.

A law that reflects more a psychological process than simply an empirical observation of the facts, the scumbling of memory over time and the dulling factor of familiarity, wherein lie the repetitive, mechanical beginnings of habit; that inexorable exorcist of adventure.

Everest may well prove the exception to this rule, in spite of being, in the language of some Alpine pundits, 'an easy rock peak'.

But at this extreme altitude the usual terms do not apply, we venture here beyond experience. Stepping into the unknown is simply a naked act of faith. All begins to tremble in the balance . . . I feel it as the very quick of life itself.

Sometimes I wonder if I'll end up going the same way as Mummery, our first apostle of rock climbing, that great pioneer of the Silver Age. Our Burra Sahib, Gen. Charlie Bruce, was with him on the 1895 expedition, when he disappeared crossing the Col, between the sovereign peaks of Nanga Parbat, with his two, stalwart Ghurka companions . . . avalanched in the snow-shrouded heights.

There's no gainsaying or denying death's open and shut paradox . . . contingent and necessary . . . everything leads to it in the end; our one certainty so slipshod on chance.

Better to think of Mummery looking down from the Matterhorn, after climbing the Zmutt arête, popping his bottle of Bouvier. Mummery always climbed prepared.

I don't see myself as making history. It would be preposterous to do so . . . Besides this intensely lived and living moment is too quick and vividly alive for that sober, desiccated dimension.

The pathetic difference in relation between the dried, pressed flower and the living plant in bloom . . . or the fossil and the creature. History often seems so inexorable . . . something lifeless set in stone.

I went to see Scott's widow before we left . . . God, that melancholy pall of quiet resignation, the awful embarrassed stultiloquence under the weight of all that could not be said . . . and the churning after-tide of consternation.

It's got to be all or nothing this time, I'll be too old for another attempt, and I can't put Ruth through anymore.

That springtime in heaven with Ruth, I wanted only a new vocabulary of love. Venice, the billowing flowers above Asolo and her gentle smile with that look in her soulful, almond-shaped eyes; she had the mysterious beauty of a Botticelli Madonna. But all I had to speak my love to her were the old and tired poeticisms, the common patrimony of clichés. I wanted only a tongue for the heart, much deeper words to sound my love. For in love I feel that we partake in the likeness of the Eternal.

But Ruth and I have said now so many good-byes . . . it has almost begun to have the ominous ring of some destined fate. This time I promised would be the last.

I'm getting used to carrying the extra weight of the gas apparatus, but wearing this india-rubber oxygen mask reminds me of the war, putting on those claustrophobic gas masks: the wretched smell, the sweaty stuffiness and the peculiarly disturbing look of insects; the new, technological face of war.

VII

War . . . an activity fit only for history . . . and a whole new vocabulary . . . spars, capstans, skiddering, sleighs and parbuckling . . .

All became familiar terms as I learnt the field craft of the guns, battery fire, the siege artillery formulae for use with the slide rule and the two basic roles of employing heavy artillery . . . counter-bombardment and bombardment . . . the obligatory overture to the apotheosis of Man's brutality.

On leaving Woolwich, I had it all by heart, Second Lieutenant Mallory reporting to serve King & Country. Reporting for duty in the war . . . the Great War . . . the war to end all wars.

It was 1916 . . . conscription began . . . and daylight saving time came in . . . along with Mott's *Theory of Shell Shock* . . . and we had a new word . . . *barrage*.

Dashing conceptions of a war of manoeuvres were now mired in the real war of attrition. The creeping barrage was the order of the day. I was assigned to a

Siege Artillery Battery dug in north-east of Albert. How can I ever forget the indescribable bouquet and the weltering mire of all that nightmarish mud?

And the magnificent cacophony of big guns . . . no symphony should be complete without it, but the interminable bloody waiting, the *longueurs infini de la guerre* . . .

How we frittered away the hours . . . sorting through piles of discarded, old socks to see if we could make up any good pairs. Who could forget the Iliad joys of army life . . . never mind whizz-bangs or 'The Big Push', this was a world where every sock counted, and socks, damn it, had to be fit for heroes.

Such Stoic training in the art of patience. Nothing can beat a good war for exacting lessons in patience. How I learnt to praise the benison of bed. G.H.Q. should have written a pamphlet, 'Rules For The Sober Fortitude Of Those Who Prefer Excitement'.

But the man who wants excitement should make it his business to beware the tedium of historic events. History is no place for the impatient. I sent home for my climbing boots.

They were ideal for 'Fathom Five', the forward O.P. dug-out, along with *The Spirit of Man,* my binoculars, director and one-man, Barr & Stroud range-finder, all ready to pin point the enemy . . . to direct the guns on to the target at the precise angle.

'Always take three observations and give the mean range'. The perils, joys, boredom and excitement of 'O. Pipping', and no 'early schools' to take . . . almost worth a war for that alone, but I never saw myself as a soldier.

It was, however, so much safer, even at Charterhouse, to teach history rather than live it. But as one old C.O. said to me: 'War is just like life old chap, I'm afraid it's a terribly mixed bag'. And that is the motley of history.

I couldn't believe in Hegel's vision of history, that reason is the sovereign of the world, that the history of the world presents us with a rational process. I looked across a world of madness.

There was Count Moltke's dictum: 'War is an element in the order of the world ordained by god'. But I didn't believe in its divine ordinance . . . only in my training in the art of ordnance. 'Artillery preparation' . . . Alexander the Great's invention.

Even now I can see the gun emplacements . . . sitting cowled under her camouflage netting, No.4 gun, a squat 9.2 heavy howitzer; known affectionately to gunners as a 'Mother' . . . it had the breach to deliver an inferno.

Angle of sight, range and elevation . . . all down to the square on the hypotenuse. The proverbial square on the hypotenuse. Pascal's *l'esprit de geometrique* . . . and the irreconcilable wrongness of war. You couldn't square that on the slide rule . . . and as it said in the Artillery Handbook: 'the cursor is a small German silver frame . . .'

The hateful orisons of the guns left not even a ruined choir for a rare pair of swallows to nest in. A world of mud and carnage, our new raped world fit only for rats. The nightmare landscape of our making, the inhumanity of man to man. You only find Satan in paradise.

Each week came news of old friends, gazetted now amongst the company of the dead: Rupert Brooke, Hugh Wilson, Siegfried Herford. It seemed only yesterday we picked him up at Bangor . . . our Double Girdle Traverse of Lliwedd together, the sunlit, Christmas memory of it still . . .

His climb of the central buttress of Scawfell, that achieved a new sense of what was possible; a Boche sniper got him in the head at Ypres. God, war is an unforgivable business.

Clausewitz said there could never be a geometry of war . . . in other words, no divinely exact, *a priori* choreography. H. G. Wells thought that air power, the first step to the heralding stars, promised the key to victory; tomorrow's way to the future. Man's destiny to explore the Milky Way . . . not just simply to go up the line.

I had spent some hours in anticipation . . . inspecting an anti-aircraft battery. I lifted my eyes unto the sky that day and saw the future, narrowly focussed in the cross-thread of a telescopic sight.

Unmoved that night, on the eve of the great offensive, the stars declared only their light years of mind-boggling remoteness, the godforsaken silences of infinite space. Peace be the constellation of the future. Tomorrow the 4th Army would advance. I almost believed in a bloody victory.

But day dawned like a weeping wound, the stigmata of its coming apocalypse . . . the opening of the Battle of the Somme . . . the harrowing of those hours of sacrifice . . . till nightfall came shivering finally in, to the diminuendo of the gunfire, a tide of cold comfort for the living.

Time for the vigil of flash spotting, a sharp eye, the soldiers salvation, a mind focussed on the job in hand; to keep busy sandbags the grief . . .

The understood last rite for the hosts of our dead . . .

And once again the General Staff cried: 'We want more men. WE WANT MORE MEN'. As out of the sky came strafing the *Jastas* of the *Schlachtflieger.*

Roll on, Duration . . . I thought as we ran for shelter. Ruefully I remembered reading, at such times, some classic text book words in one of the sad little volumes of Artillery Training which we'd been issued: 'such a complete lack of self-interest that he will do his duty in the hour of danger coolly and accurately'. One of the old wags had put a sign above the entrance to our dug-out: 'Remember there's a war on'.

Those periods of being under intense fire would poignantly bring back to my mind, an amusing incident I came across while researching Boswell for my biographical study. His father wanted him to enlist in the army, but the Duke of Argyll, commenting on his application to join the Guards, remarked disarmingly to his father: 'I like your son, that boy must not be shot at for three and sixpence a day'.

I was receiving seven and sixpence a week for the privilege . . . but to keep my thoughts otherwise in check, I would seize the opportunity to improve my aircraft recognition. I even saw through my binoculars a *Pfaltz* of tender blue . . . just as in the ruddy song. I almost wrote to *The Times* . . . on the question of life imitating art. A *Zeppelin* couldn't have annoyed them more.

My younger brother, Trafford, was in the R.A.F., in command then of No. 8 Squadron. He'd joined in the days of Fred Karno's Air Corps, and as they used to say in the Ragtime Flying Corps: 'Thou shalt not covet the Recording Officer's job, nor any cushy job that is his'.

Patient accuracy, clear thought, science, this I learnt from the French Artillery, studying them in action with the *153 Grande Puissance howitzer.* And the quintessence of it all . . . the *Systeme D* – 'ingenious improvisation', or simply 'initiative in overcoming difficulties'.

The application of Pascal's *l'esprit de finesse*, the spirit of intuition, therein lies the key, to use the spirit of intuition within the compass of the rigorous spirit of geometry. This is the Philosopher's Stone.

VIII

A delightful boon of serendipity, the surprising blue poppy of Tibet, happy flower of an Arcadian world: a bright poppy that doesn't bear the mournful memories of the dead. It really was such a joyous sight, the heavenly blue of celestial bliss. Its vibrant colour so redolent of the sublime *Eritrichium nanum* . . . the highest and brightest of all the blue Alpines. I love the gentle beauty of flowers.

The ground here is not so good, scree and steeply-angled rock scattered with shards of detritus, so easy to skid and scud off from. Ware the delicate foliation of ice.

Such is the magisterial height of Everest that we look down on all the other surrounding peaks . . . the inexpressible immensity of the view . . . words cannot compass this stupendous scale . . . We're already nearly as high up the mountain as our highest point in '22. This is the advantage of the 'English air' . . . the extra vim it provides. I'm almost sure I can feel the alveoli sponging up this precious oxygen.

The divine afflatus of the gas, how it slows the rate of breathing down.

The leader is the stroke of the party, and I've really set a cracking pace . . . the grim humour of that term pace for our agonising progress now. I'm just hoping Sandy is all right. Occasionally I stop to point, gesturing by hand signals or indicating with my ice axe anything to watch out for. Gesticulating in exaggerated dumbshow . . . just like Charlie Chaplin.

I cannot speak any more than he . . . we are in the kingdom of the mute . . . only the high-pressure hiss of the gas is our monotonous accompaniment.

We have no scallop shell of quiet. I only hope we have the equation of time, distance and atmospheres rightly balanced in our favour.

I told them I wanted to climb Mt. Woolworth in New York, but Harold Lloyd beat me to it, in crazy comic style, in *Safety Last,* climbing that skyscraper in Los Angeles. One of the best films I've seen, funnier than *Easy Street.* Even I couldn't have matched his antic, droll technique, that hair-raising daftness and the death defying pirouettes. Such hare-brained stunts are best left to the professionals.

I earnt $700 less than Conan Doyle on my lectures in the U.S.A. . . . elementary

Watson . . . you can't compete with fictional heroes . . . and any climbing leader could learn from Sherlock Holmes . . . practitioner of the art of perception raised to the preternatural.

But here I am appearing now on film, who'd have thought it, climbing for the edification and entertainment of the public. I hate the idea of it . . . it makes me feel like a circus performer.

I remember that grousing, old curmudgeon, Lt. Col. Strutt, an insufferably opinionated, porridge-with-salt-man, upon reaching the top of the North Col saying: "I wish that bloody cinema was here, if I look anything like what I feel, I ought to be immortalised for the British public".

Let's hope I have the darn luck of Buster Keaton, or the infinite capacity to cheat fate like Harold Lloyd. But Noel is making an epic, *The Epic of Mount Everest.* I think he'd like to have me coming down, not with the 'Ten Commandments', that's old hat now, but with a ghoulish, Tibetan devil or two, suitably wearing necklaces of human skulls.

After all, the public's currently agog with Tutankhamun: Noel's cinematograph of the expedition has to compete.

And so do I, against the last, snowy, inhospitable heights of Everest; such is 'the masquerade of the changeling nicknamed Free Will'.

But I've no choice just this minute . . . I've simply got to stop and rest a while. Sometimes it's quite impossible not to admire the view . . .

Below me the great sweep of winding glaciers; slow, irresistible, crystalline rivers of glistering ice, and the landscape in its bleak state of glacial denudation. I'm reminded of climbing on Tryfan, looking down and into Cwm Idwal, it was there Charles Darwin perceived that the overgrown mounds in the cwm, were moraines left by retreating glaciers . . . glaciers die of hunger for snow.

It's curious to think that mighty glaciers, such as these, once ground and grinded in an ice-bound age over much of Great Britain, that our own mountains were sculpted by glaciers. The 'Glacial Epoch' in Prof. Agassiz's phrase, 'a period in the history of our planet . . .'

It was some time though before Agassiz's vision came to be generally accepted, the signature of the parallel roads of Glen Roy and the mountain of the evidence were not enough. A fundamental shift in mental climate, often seems to require a near geological time span . . . as if it had the same, slow rhythm as a landscape.

Although the geologist Charles Lyell was initially sceptical, Agassiz's envisioning of an ice age was Lyellian in its attempt to explain former changes to the Earth's surface by reference to causes now in operation.

It was an illustration of Lyell's own insightful doctrine: 'The present is the key to the past, the past is the key to the present'. There is the true, Janus face of comprehension that sets the living pulse of real understanding.

Though neither Agassiz nor Lyell its inspirer accepted Darwin's Theory of Evolution . . . Lyell always said that he couldn't 'go the whole Orang'. Our deeply ingrained attitudes do not evolve over time . . . they make dinosaurs of us in the end.

I'm looking way across at Mt. Clare . . . with its magnificent High Gothic architecture, that fantastic ridge of cornices and towers, and the almost perfect pyramid of its perpetual, snow-dreaming spire. It's such a beautiful mountain, so I named it after my daughter. The R.G.S. wouldn't let the name stand, so it's officially on the map as Pumori, which does, at least, mean daughter peak.

I look at mountains geometrically, somewhat in the manner of a cubist, as Plato observed, 'god ever geometrizes'; geometry was my first love at school. Discovering Geoffrey had a similar eye, I threatened, only half in jest, to write a critical piece for the *Alpine Journal*. Promising to fully unmask the cubist movement in orosophy, adumbrating briefly, in outline, how it had anticipated Braque and Picasso.

Later, I learnt that Braque had said that he and Picasso, were like two mountaineers roped together . . . the closest bond of men exploring the unknown.

The sun is beginning to burnish the snow, so it's time to put my snow goggles on and get moving again . . .

Climbing in the green filtered world now of the goggles, in their curious submarine air . . . clambering up what was once a sea floor. The past is the key to the present.

Diastrophism . . . regions sink and regions rise, as so do the reputations of men, subject as they are too to the weathering and erosion of time.

The rocks are treacherously covered in a shivered cascade of brash, imagine a kind of lithic dandruff. This continual scaling-off from the rock collects in all the crannies and crevices, into scree casts of mutual attrition. It makes a damned awkward terrain . . . you have to watch your footing constantly. And it's made even more difficult now, with the narrow view field of the goggles.

At moments like this you can really savour the wry humour of Donald Robertson's remark, 'climbers are always trying in self-defence to maintain the fiction that they are enjoying themselves'.

Mummery was surely right in his observation that 'the essence of the sport, lies not in ascending a peak, but in struggling with and overcoming difficulties . . .'

And that's just how Pater summed up the pleasure of writing, 'the delightful sense of difficulties overcome' . . . the feeling of delight in it . . .

People are always asking me to explain or justify the sport of climbing . . . but climbing, just like life itself, has no narrow rational purpose . . . all its sense lies in the doing.

The feeling of delight in it . . . in the current of alert senses . . . the intensely lived concentration, nerved with its fraught exhilaration, burning off the accretion of routine, the quotidian layers of sedimentation.

A reawakening to what it means to be alive, the unaccountable miraculousness of being . . . and that feeling of sheer delight in it.

Even on an expedition such as this, there are times when one has to consciously resist the easy, complicit fall into the mechanical way of doing things; the unconscious illapse into the robot state.

That condition of 'Rossum's Universal Robots'. 'Robots are not life. Robots are machines.'

The mechanical is an all unthinking grind, our humanity often needs startling back into life . . . so that it quivers heartfelt into being again.

Damn, I almost lost my footing . . . a salutary reminder . . . 'Right Mindfulness'. As they used to say, in the early days of guideless climbing, 'the Englishman likes to find his own way to heaven'. You have to be your own angel.

I've always loved those lines of Emily Brontë's:

> I'll walk where my own nature would be leading–
> It vexes me to choose another guide–

And my own heart too inclines to 'where the wild wind blows on the mountainside'.

Though Dr. Johnson wrote about mountains disparagingly, he thought 'their uniformity and barrenness could afford little amusement to the traveller', but he did, at least, recognise that 'he who mounts the precipices has a kind of turbulent pleasure, between fright and admiration'.

He didn't get quite as far as Herford's 'ecstasy that thrills the blood', but then the Doctor's understanding of climbing was a steep walk.

It was Gray who was the first to cultivate an aesthetic appreciation of 'those monstrous creatures of God . . . pregnant with religion and poetry'. Only much later would Ruskin reverentially write, 'the mountains of the earth are its natural cathedrals'.

Though Ruskin was horrified at the idea of climbing them, to make a vulgar playground of the virgin, Alpine snows: 'one would as soon think of climbing the pillars of the choir at Beauvais for a gymnastic exercise'.

But as Sandy quipped to the reporters: 'It's the duty of the Alpine Club to climb as near as it can to Heaven'.

And today we'll climb as far as this great vault of the white crested Earth goes to heaven . . . up even through the choir of the wind, scaling the heights along the North-east Ridge.

It was a North-east Ridge that led Whymper to the pristine peak of the Matterhorn, that legendary summit of the Golden Age.

It was his ninth attempt . . . this is my third. In reply to the chorus of 'what's-the-users', I'm reminded of Rutherford's toast at the annual Cavendish Laboratory dinner: "To the electron . . . may it never be of use to anyone".

And may Everest hold its own with the electron.

IX

I'm beginning to get a good view now of the first rock step. And the issue of whether we will be able to surmount it, and gain the crest of the ridge remains to be decided. I had some severe doubts here, yesterday afternoon, about it being a realistic possibility. But we'll see, soon enough, if it is a feasible option.

Odell, our geologist, is keen to get information about the palaeontological character of the rocks. To determine whether they are fossiliferous and he's rather hoping to collect one or two specimens containing fossils . . . those haunting relics of former living things . . . the casual, testamentary heirlooms of evolution.

So he wants us to keep an eye out for any sign of fossils . . . crinoids, brachiopods and lamellibranches. And even better still, gastropods and ammonites.

To find a crinoid on the summit and know that you stand on a fossil bed of sea lillies. Or exhume from the aeons a fossil snail shell . . . to discover that you've been anticipated by a palaeological gastropod . . . Or maybe a petrified nautiloid that once wandered the Palaeozoic currents . . . the ancestor of the pearly Nautilus in your hand.

Perhaps make the discovery, in the limestone shale, that this once was rugose coral that forms the summit . . . that the goddess wears a fossil coronet of coral.

I did find a fossil near the summit of Y Garn once; a small, rusty coloured outline of a shell, the imprint of its whorls preserved in the rock. It turned out to be a brachiopod.

And it was such a comfort to hear that teeth and bones are readily fossilizable. Good to know that posterity has something to get its hands on . . . you can see it squinting at a molar. Dentition bears enduring witness.

X

My new boots have stood up well, they're Dewberry's not Carter's Dreadnoughts . . . on this steeply angled rock so much can depend on the friction of one's boot nails.

Even with all the layers of clothing I've got on it's still bloody, damn chilly . . . in spite of my new, warm, woollen waistcoat.

I hate waistcoats . . . they're so fuddy-duddy, the old, dry-as-dust beaks wore them at school . . . a cynosure of pedantry . . . enough to put anyone off for life. But at high altitude one needs the extra body warmth they provide, so Ruth kindly knitted me a rather stylish one, in an 'arty', William Morris pattern.

I didn't much care for the leather Expedition issue ones, they were unaesthetic . . . that drear drabness of uniform . . . so utterly cheerless.

XI

Although it's a distinctive feature of the skyline of the North-east ridge, this initial rock step is not a very big or impressive outcrop, but it is our first, potentially major obstacle. The rucked and weathered rock configuration of it, looms large and imminent above us now, forming the bulk of our horizon . . . as we continue climbing steadily up towards it . . . at this arduous slog . . . slowly climbing . . . climbing up.

As that great author, Anonymous, in the introduction to *The Roof-Climber's Guide To Trinity* says: 'In these athletic days of rapid devolution to the Simian practices of our ancestors, climbing is naturally assuming an ever more prominent position'. The Everest expeditions have really caught the public imagination. So now our slow, exacting steps are seen as being in the vanguard of the march of progress . . . that seductive, perennial illusion.

But on this march, the going is such that one is forced to admire the view, a little more often than is strictly correct . . . but as Dante discovered in his *Purgatory:* 'to look back is wont to cheer climbing men'.

The play of light and shadow on the mountains . . . the way my thought and mood shift in relief . . .

I would like to have been a poet . . . I've always loved poetry, that ancient, word-woven charm against the perennial forgetfulness of men.

Poetry is the sublime contexture of words, the arresting play of resonant images that strike the inner chords of our being . . . moving us in the depths as the view now.

Martin Conway is right, 'it's not Nature that illuminates the mind, but the mind that glorifies nature. The beauty that we behold must first arise in ourselves'. He asks men not to understand mountains, but to understand themselves by means of mountains.

'To struggle and to understand . . . never this last without the other'. And as the philosopher Moore has shown, the act of knowing requires a mental act and an object independent of that act.

This is the essence of our engagement with the *real* . . . and more deeply with the nature of ourselves: the way we become more intensely present . . . more *there* . . . there in the still quick of being itself . . . where the rhythms of life, rock and snow are movements in an underscored harmony.

And to the mountain now in Shelley's words:

The secret strength of things
which governs thought, and to the infinite dome
Of Heaven, inhabits thee

Einstein's $E = MC^2$ . . . the interrelationship of mass and energy . . . rock, snow, cloud and mind . . . forms of the underlying, seamless pattern.

As the jewelled glints and diamond glister scintillant now in the snow.

XII

Well, we're in the shadow of the rock step and my oxygen is running out . . . that's it . . . that's my first cylinder gone. It's the welcome chance to jettison some weight. I've got to smartly unclip and take my oxygen mask off now and wait for Sandy. And just breathe this thin, high altitude air as deeply as I can. Taking deep breaths, using my whole diaphragm, filling the lungs to maximum capacity, in a capacious trawl for scarce oxygen.

Switching over to a new oxygen bottle, is still an awkward, unhandy operation, in spite of Sandy's inversion of the bottles. I'll need his help to manage the change over; it's a damn, fiddly business adjusting the apparatus. And I'm too chary and cack-handed, to begin to tackle it myself with any confidence. I don't have Sandy's mechanical knack and deftness, the natural feel for these things. And this needs the sure touch of the man who really knows what he's doing.

All this new-fangled gadgetry making life easier . . . and the expertise it requires . . . but our climb would be hopeless without it. It all comes down in the end to Sandy's savvy.

After the monotonous hiss of the oxygen, the plainsong of the wind comes as a relief. We'll stop here for coffee; thirst is the real trial at altitude. You can never carry enough thermos flasks.

There's always the easy temptation to justify what we're doing by claiming it has some scientific value . . .

Our Everest Expeditions have led to the discovery of two, new fleas, hitherto entirely unknown to science, a new species of Pika (*Ochotona wollastoni*); a scuttle of more than 300 hundred beetles of Palaearctic distribution, not forgetting our stick-insect, plus a delightful, new genus of butterflies. And to the discovery of Norton's Toad, which has webbed toes.

Sightings of Guldenstadt's Redstart & Adam's mountain-finch have kept the ornithologist in our group generally excited. And we've found little Attid spiders mysteriously surviving up to 22,000ft but, so far, not a single mollusc has been found, so we we're all issued with pill-boxes and told to be on the lookout.

And it is hoped that the gentle Dr. Hingston will shoot a native species of wren, in the interests of science, of course, for comparative ornithological research. Poor *Troglodytes troglodytes* . . . I suggested a gallant miss for the honour of *Homo sapiens* . . . that dubious, rapacious parvenu.

We weren't allowed to bring Heron, our previous geologist, back with us. His enthusiasm for dynamite and exploratory rock explosions was, according to the local Tibetans, disturbing the demons that sleep under the sacred mountains. And it's a wise man who respects and leaves sleeping demons to dream.

We've also managed to establish two, new height records, once again, but I don't want to make any more altitude records this time. We're actually drinking this coffee above the highest point of my last record . . . such is the relativity of a record.

It's easy to picture Younghusband here, on his quest for natural beauty, of 'holiness itself made manifest', wrapped in his *Rumpur Chuddur,* with a mug of Liebig's soup in his hand: 'a grim old apostle of adventure'.

I'm turning in to face the mountainside, kicking my boots against the rocks to keep the circulation going in my toes. It's nice to get back with toes . . . all of your toes on your feet.

I'll treat myself to some more tepid coffee as well . . . the simple luxuries . . . they're the ones that really count. The ones that come in answer to our shorn and tempered prayers. And, by god, they make us truly grateful.

Dr. Hingston has been studying the physiological effects of altitude on us, subjecting us all to a battery of tests to measure and record the decline in our faculties . . . the arithmetic one . . . 'a test of brain liveliness' . . . is by far the most popular.

I take a secret, childish delight in coming top of the arithmetic tests, it's absurd I know and not very grown up at all; a childish competitiveness that takes me back to prep school days at Glengorse. Happy memories of the comfort and solace of my geometry books.

Our great regret was not having a botanist among the Expedition members, especially during 'the great rhododendron march' . . . we really needed a Joseph Hooker.

It's time to open the flow-valve on the new cylinder and put my oxygen mask back on . . . I feel more like a diver, sealed off in a world narrowly submerged in green, drowned in the closed in sound of my own breathing.

Sandy redesigned this oxygen apparatus from the impossible contraption Siebe Gorman supplied; 'boggled' was how Sandy succinctly summed it up. And he's made it possible to use it, climbing up on rock, with a less 'Agag-like' delicacy in Norton's phrase.

So Sandy's toolbox has been worth its weight in gold . . . without his technical skill and engineering wizardry we couldn't have made a gas attempt, we would have had no real chance of the summit.

Even with the oxygen, the going is so much harder than I thought . . . it's as if this high altitude air leaches out one's energy by osmosis . . .

This is proving to be the most exacting effort . . . Everest, my god, is one hell of a bugger. But, heavens above! A new frontier of the possible . . . God, help us . . .

XIII

The actuality of the first rock step has proved something of a disappointment, I've seen enough of it now to have my suspicions confirmed. Our plan to go up the skyline, simply isn't a practicable route.

The crest of the ridge, above the rock step, is covered in about twenty to thirty feet of wind-honed, iced compact snow, like a giant piping of icing sugar, right the way up to the towering, brute bulk of the second rock step above. Quite impossible . . . so we're going to turn this obstacle on the right and traverse, following the line Norton and Somervell took.

I'm really not that sorry, the view I had just back there, from the top of the ridge, of the sheer drop down to the Kangshung glacier, was unnervingly awesome. And I've got an angel's head for heights . . . but I am wanting the miracle of wings. It was no place to get caught by the wind.

XIV

I compared a day in the Alps to a great symphony and likened the mountaineer to an artist . . . that did and may still strike some people as absurd. My article was greeted with a chorus of brickbats and plaudits, but neither of the parties got the point . . . and it was 1914 . . . the year all the world was so busily going to war.

I was really speaking of the shared, core experience . . . that when the climber's individual sense is submerged, yet his consciousness of himself is more alert and heightened, he comes to a more profound realisation of himself. And that is my understanding of the aesthetic experience . . . and the moment when the dancer and the dance become one.

But climbing isn't all rhythm and harmony by any means; it has its jarring discords between the mind and body, its interminable mental fugues, the maniacal monologues, and its scatological, scrannel notes of dissatisfaction. Spleen finds its natural channel in Anglo-Saxon imprecation . . . our necessary vein of bloody-mindedness that helps to give a precarious purchase on the rough-grain of adversity.

Notwithstanding those drear days of unrelieved purgatory, the hills all muffled round with sodden clouds, the cursed rock intractable and the interminable rain running down your neck, I still feel that something sublime is the essence of climbing . . . It is my art . . . though there are times, now to be precise, when I wonder if I shouldn't have followed the example of the Master, Henry James, and been 'just literary'. It has always been my ambition to write . . . to cast the fine spell of words . . .

As it is my climbing articles have generally met with the response: 'never mind what you thought about the mountain, tell us how you climbed it'. I'm considered far too literary in some quarters.

I've always been more interested in the spiritual journey that accompanies a climb . . . and in the chance afforded 'To cleanse the Face of my Spirit by Self-examination'.

Only this time I've been more troubled and concerned with the tensions surrounding the decision to come out, once again, on an Everest expedition: for yet one more chance of a lifetime . . . to be weighed against the personal cost . . . 'but how could I be out of the hunt'.

Wells, in his *Outline of History,* suggests that the pattern of the evolution of human history is to be seen in the conflict between the settled, agrarian civilisations, that created tradition and lived by tradition, and the influx and conquests of nomadic tribesman.

'Today the power of tradition is destroyed, the body of our state is civilisation still, but its spirit is that of the nomadic world'. Wells sees in the boldness of scientific enquiry and the universal restlessness of our times, the evidence of the 'nomadisation' of civilisation.

It is a pattern seen in the fire . . . a prophet's making sense . . .

And H.G. would, of course, have us be nomads, navigating the star swarms, on our destined odyssey, by ever new and remoter constellations of stars, crossing the vast regions of inhospitable space . . . argonauts of the dust lanes in the starry heavens.

But it's a vision that allows me to make some sense of the inner conflict within myself. The two halves of my character, the part that longs to stay at home with Ruth, see the children growing up, and the other part of me, the nomadic half, that finds that stifling after a while. For whom that gentle, cosy, loving world is not enough, and in my soft, psychic innards I find that shocking . . . a painful rift tearing at the very heart of me.

Though I think this fundamental dichotomy is in the essential nature of our being. Something more primeval than Wells understands . . . I think that it's primordial, the *ur* condition of mankind . . . a natural systole and diastole of the psyche . . . the two cross-currents of the heart's desire . . . which we experience as the soul's ceaseless, warring, internal quarrel . . .

But perhaps I'm falling here now into self-justification . . . arguing disingenuously from my own, individual case to the universal. But we see the world only in and through our personal history, in the highlight and relief of memory, our uniquely lived and living history.

A history that, just like this mountain range, can be seen as a landscape shifting according to the light of the present and the perspective. Though, on reflection, it might be truer, to say that we see the world most deeply, in the alchemical light of our imagination.

The imagination sets the reach of vision in the mind . . . without imagination we could not realise the possible . . . conceive of concepts beyond the bounds of received wisdom. And in our present age this appears so vital, as we seem bereft . . . left upon a darkling plain . . . struggling to 'think God's thoughts after him' . . . to understand Creation. Or fathom a more austere comfort, in an understanding of a Universe that is divine in all but godliness and even more occult in mystery.

Just imagine what heights remain . . .

XV

My real and only concern now is reaching the summit, nothing else . . . nothing has the same magnitude of reality . . . all else is insubstantial gossamer beside its dominating presence. I've put too much of myself into this effort to give up at this stage. Besides, it's the only real chance I've had and there won't be another.

The slow, painstaking task of traversing along and up treacherous, very steep sloping ground is a particularly exacting business; it's treadmill work, but you have to really concentrate all the time. And the Everest sedimentary series begins to pall interminably.

The patience of Job is the absolutely necessary qualification . . . that and undaunted perseverance. You have to forswear the pleasures of mountaineering to take on the highest mountain; this is a medieval penance.

What shall I tell you? Tales, marvellous tales . . .

We were followed up to our high camps by ravens, they have the sinister air of being death's harbingers . . . but reminded me of Snowdon, standing on Yr Wydffa, watching the ravens circling below over dark Glaslyn. The dead, cirque lake that gives you an uncanny feeling, and with the ravens a cauldron's brew of atmosphere.

The crags repeat the raven's croak
in symphony austere . . .

Romantic Wales . . . land of King Arthur and O. G. Jones. That journeyman climb of his, Milestone Buttress Ordinary . . . the road from Bangor was never quite the same after. And his book, *Rock Climbing in the English Lake District,* the analytic classification of the four grades of difficulty; Easy, Moderate, Difficult and Exceptionally Severe. The shaping and pioneering of modern British rock climbing: immortalised in those photographs by the Abraham brothers.

And I'm very conscious now of his observation, that a line must be drawn somewhere, to separate the possible from the impossible . . . some try to draw it by their own experience.

It's a line that boasts no breadth . . . the line that separates the difficult from the dangerous, as Whymper said, is a true line without breadth.

A line without breadth, as mysterious as an infinitesimal, but sharper than Occam's razor . . . the Whymper line. And it can be alarmingly easy to pass and very hard to see, 'it's sometimes passed unconsciously . . . the consciousness that it has been passed is felt too late'. The chilling prospect . . .

That rising panic in the pit of your stomach, coming with the awful realisation that you might be going the way of the infinitesimal . . . to become the ghost of a departed quantity. One must be mindful of the Whymper line, if adventure is not to become a wanton risk of life. We come to the mountains to live life more intensely . . . to be in the full current of the concentration of our vital senses . . . not to die but to experience the marrow of our being . . .

But danger shadows adventure in direct relation, the degree of one is the measure of the other.

From the beginning think what may be the end . . .

We must be moving on . . . onwards and upwards . . . up to those rocks at the base of the rock step. I'm keeping a weather eye on the summit, as Keats said, 'there is nothing more fickle than the top of a mountain' . . . and it's our weathervane.

I've taken a copy of Keats's *Letters* out with me, to read in quiet moments on the Expedition. And what has struck me most deeply, so far, is Keats's conception of the world as 'The Vale of Soulmaking'. A world with the grain, its causal texture, set to generate the kindling action of Heart and Mind on each other for the purpose of forming Soul . . .

A necessary, tutelary world of pain and suffering, instressing intelligence to crystallise intricately into an implex sense of self-identity: the haecceity of our being, the taste of ourselves. That and the Buddha's insight that this is the source of all our suffering, that only when we have transcended the confines of our personal identity, managed to lose this separate taste of ourselves, do we realise the 'immortal diamond' within and attain enlightenment.

Out of the larval stage of our desires, to form a chrysalis for the ego . . . patient for the miracle of selflessness . . . the opening all within . . . putting off, in Blake's words, 'all that is not of god alone'.

But I cannot climb yet out of my ambition, my desire, the obscure sense of duty and some unconscious need that keeps me climbing up the mountainside. What I do is me . . . the way I find expression . . . this activity that quickens the feel of life; my deepest sense of being is in climbing . . . wherein I find the composure of my soul.

Enlightenment is further from me than the summit . . . I know only the hunger for that larger compassing of the understanding, but in climbing there is deep fulfilment . . . and afterwards the profound feeling of serenity. To lose oneself in the concentration of climbing that brings out the veins of one's reality, clearing the mind's focus from the film of mundane familiarity, this is the nearest I get to Nirvana.

So as a spiritual pilgrim, I inevitably fall all too humanly short of the Buddha and William Blake. But it was by reading Blake's visionary work *Milton,* exposing hypocritical holiness in all its oppressiveness . . . the inhumanity that lord's it in the self-righteous guise of moral virtue . . . and in and through his shining vision of 'Milton the Awakener . . . upon England's mountains green . . . in fearless majesty annihilating Self' . . . announcing 'I in my Selfhood am that Satan; I am that Evil One! He is my Spectre!' That's how I came to what understanding I have of the awakened Buddha.

'The Eternal Great Humanity, seen in every face as the breath of the Almighty' . . . or as manifestations of the Buddha . . . and the mystic's path which sees the selfhood as an incrustation over the immortal spirit or Buddha nature that must be 'put off and annihilated alway'. All travellers to eternity pass inward . . .

XVI

Now, to the exigent concerns of the present, the immediate demands of the traverse of this pitch: a very awkward and exposed route, over broken, discontinuous ledges, that run along the tops of steeply angled slabs of rock. And some are covered still with a powdering of fine, powdery snow. Making it even more awkward . . . and taxing on the nerves. It's the nearest damn thing to tightrope walking at times. Though the occasional view down to the glacier below, is certainly sufficient to concentrate the mind.

The going here is difficult . . . and the character of the rock has changed. We're on a band of yellow quartz . . . quartz has a deservedly evil reputation . . . it's slippery and apt to fracture . . . a precarious ground altogether . . . while the dry, powdery snow makes things a damn sight worse . . . concealing and treacherous . . . and it sometimes needs clearing off . . . an annoyingly time consuming business . . . nearly as bad as that bloody gardening one has to do on Lliwedd . . . And it calls for a very, consciously aware balancing act all the time. Norton was right about the sense of exposure you feel in the place. No protection to be had at all. A slip or misstep here would be fatal. I put a certain faith in Alpine nails . . . but not too many, they conduct the cold. How the soul is inescapably earthbound. We are not made for the heavens.

Mercifully now, I'm almost accustomed to the extra weight of the gas apparatus, but I dislike the feel of this clammy oxygen mask over my face. It's a real godsend though, that the high-pressure tube feeds through under my right arm, so I haven't the constant worry of it snagging, and breaking on the rocks. The real problem . . . when we get there . . . will be to regain the ridge . . . gain the route to the summit.

In profile Sandy, with his pith helmet and oxygen mask on, looks as if he is wearing a bizarre, medieval helmet, a cross between a salade and a snout-faced basinet

. . . like some weird, futuristic myrmidon or angel of nemesis.
Against the wind we both have on our armour of 3-ply gaberdine, Shackleton windproofs: the great, Antarctic explorer's legacy. Shackleton always carried a pocket Browning, a small volume of the verse not an automatic; he was Vice Chairman of the Poetry Society. His recent sad death marked the ending of an era.

So much of the adventure has gone out of the world . . . in our modern age of the wireless and the aeroplane.

Thou hast conquered, soulless industrialisation,
Dully with all thy faceless, steering committees,
The tunnel vision of thy ministering accountants,
Ushering in an homogenous and grey civilisation.

The egregious Hinks and the Everest Committee . . .

Will the paladins of the future really be committee men?

The chairman of our committee, Sir Francis Younghusband, sees great spiritual significance in the climbing of Everest, a renewal of the 'spirit of adventure', a symbolic affirmation of the spirit of man, the triumph of the spirit over matter.

But in this time of great disillusionment after the war, impatient with the old and discredited order, aching still with the heartbreak of irredeemable loss, when everything now seems questionable, our discontents require political solutions, not symbolic gestures.

The enormous task of reconstruction, but to comprehend and plan a vital reconstitution with the language still of the past and party faction, and where there is no vision . . . the future has no illumination. The 'Man with the Hoe' still holds his admonition . . . the dread shape of humanity betrayed. It's all too easy to despair of the World's condition, but our century must find a balance in the equation, between the House of Have and the House of Want . . . and put away its tribal totems of race and nation.

XVII

Geoffrey first mentioned Everest to me on Lliwedd, we were doing the Roof Route together that Easter, and having finished the 50ft central chimney, we were smoking our pipes on Birch-Tree Terrace. The tops of the hills were muffled in sloomy, grey clouds and I kept thinking wryly of Archer Thomson's phrase in the guidebook, 'Lliwedd is the Mecca for climbers'.

Everest seemed too fantastic at first to take seriously, besides nobody knew precisely where it was even, nor if men could survive in the thin air at this altitude. And, after all, how could I possibly give up my job, leaving wife and family, for such a madcap adventure.

I had no idea how Everest would come to possess me . . .

Who knows, perhaps in time Everest will be the Mecca.

XVIII

I've always seen the experience of a climb as a whole, an organic unity. And as Moore says in *Principia Ethica,* the value of a whole is neither identical with nor proportional to the sum of its parts.

And there is the fundamental paradox of life . . .

The irreducible, organic wholeness and its mysterious, inenarrable inbeing that eludes the net of rationality.

Life is a quintessential coalescence, an indissoluble, emergent harmony . . . a tonic and maddening air.

XIX

Our progress now is forestalled by a great, defensive bulwark, an enormous outcrop of rock, an up-splintered shoulder blade shrugged up by the mountain; a rebuffing, minatory *gendarme.* We've reached the ruck of rocks at the base of the second rock step. A sentinel bastion of beetling, dark grey limestone, shaped like a Dreadnought's prow, and largely disadorned of snow.

It doesn't look technically insuperable, nor as forbidding as Clogwyn Du'r Arddu, but at this altitude it's an intimidating obstacle. And cumbered with the extra weight of the sets it presents a bloody awkward problem, one that could prove insurmountable.

The judgement now of Mallory . . .

To leave it unhazarded, take Norton's route and go round to ascend via the couloir, shades of the return to the 'gully epoch', or endeavour now to gain the crest of the ridge, make trial of it, try our luck and skill to the utmost . . .

But have we the reserve of strength? We're neither of us A1. For the unknowable we must still keep our margin of strength. O, the irresolution wherein I dither . . . the risks that one might take oneself . . . I prefer difficult rock to snow . . . if only Sandy had some Alpine experience.

That so much can depend on the outcome of one tactical decision . . .

Among indifferent, arduous rocks '& snows of doubt & reasoning' . . .

To simply turn it now on the right, following the natural line of the rock and put our trust in . . . trust in . . .

The couloir . . . rough conduit of shivered, off-cast rock, the natural runnel of addled detritus, with its insidious stale bib of ice glazed snow . . . promising a dicey, hazardous ascent round its underlying bed of loose rubble.

But it's such an obvious temptation . . . in spite of possible stone falls . . . like all couloirs it looks invitingly easy, superficially the most promising route. I'm not too proud to ascend via the gutter, needs must when time is of the essence. But you can put little trust in a couloir . . . it's not the steps to *Parnassus* . . . it's really just the place for a *Boojum.*

I said in '21 that much would depend upon the possibility of escaping from the ridge to avoid obstacles and on our being able to regain it again. I wonder now though if we can regain the ridge after traversing round into the couloir, only Norton's judgement to go on, but his poor eyes could already have been affected, there's no time now to reconnoitre.

And as he reports the couloir is blocked with unconsolidated, powdery snow, that makes the thought of a descent back down it an unwelcome prospect. Besides our attempt could flounder for hours, stymied in the tricky, blind maze of it, with vitally precious time frittered away, the opportunity of the summit wasted. Something about its siren, easy look gives me a bad feeling about it . . . shades of Sir Galahad and the Grail . . . the seductive fascination of the seemingly easy forever luring one away from the right path . . .

And isn't there always a chink in the dragon's armour?

Let's start to look for cracks in the rock, the natural fault lines in its defences. 'It's only difficult if it's not impossible'. I knew I would have to pick up the gauntlet. Only if learned Mallory will be resolute will danger wink on opportunity . . .

The mountaineer as calculated gambler, with only such artistry as he has to rely on. At least this way we can say we put up a fight, that we did come to grips with the mountain. *Fortissimo* at last . . .

Anyway, it will be a welcome relief to finally get to use one's arms. Now for the moment of scapulimancy . . .

I think I can see a route that might go, something like a triple knight's move. We won't be able to manage this climbing encumbered with the oxygen apparatus, the crucial question is whether we'll have the breath to climb without it.

It has always been my pet plan to climb the mountain gasless, only the sheer, brutal reality of it disabused me. But this short stretch might be physically possible to achieve.

Deprived of the 'English air' we can only rely now on the inspiriting of *L'Energie Spirituel* . . . what that inspiring, Indian lawyer, Ghandi, calls '*satyagraha*' . . . soul-force. It's down to naked soul-force . . . '*satyagraha*', let's hope the mountain will honour fair means.

Moderate rock but in this rarefied air will I be able to breathe sufficiently for such a concerted muscular effort. I'm just closing the flow-valve off on the oxygen and now removing my oxygen mask. A few moments to adjust . . . and take the air . . . allowing the body time to switch over to '*satyagraha*'.

Unburdened now and appreciably lightened . . . it feels almost a reprieve . . . a deliverance to get the handicapping weight of the oxygen set off.

And all the doubt was now – should I be fit . . .

This thin air dulls the mental atmosphere of the play of quick, compounded thought, it numbs the motive power of the will . . . a subtly insidious erosion of the inscape.

And it's too tricky to judge the rock through my snow goggles; it requires a naked eye reading to get the detail of the pitch. Then I have to pace it out mentally.

Not badly exfoliated, no treacherous bands of quartz, the rock is sound, it's only difficult because of the altitude . . . the terrible strain on lungs at their absolute limits. This is no Eagles Nest Ridge Direct and yet, I'm quietly taking stock. Studying the physiognomy of the rock, the inclination of the strata, picking out holds afforded by clefts and crannies, each serendipitous excrescence, sighting vital, enabling burrs, selecting the surest line.

Think first . . . climb afterwards . . . And the climbing leader must always bear in mind what the man behind can do, as much as what he can achieve himself . . . the symbiotic nature of the rope of two.

The goggles restrict my field of vision, I'll feel more secure climbing without them, even at the risk to my eyes. So I'll call this awkward, diagonal pitch Exposure beyond the Visible Spectrum. I'll have to move very quickly though . . . otherwise I'll end up as snow-blind as Norton.

The only protection here will be foresight, a sound reading of the line of holds ahead and a steady nerve . . . the bedrock of a calm unruffled judgement.

Time to remove the thick, warm gloves and strip down to my climbing mittens . . .

The feel of bare fingers on naked rock . . .

I move on the tractable knurls of its veins . . .

The rocks are so cold they feel sticky, my finger pads adhere to their surface and I leave a thin layer of skin behind in the parting, blistering my fingertips.

The rocks exact their forfeit of flesh, so each time, I pay for my pains.

And through my winged words . . .

just leavened with the odd oath.

XX

The redemptive energy in a forceful expletive . . . I'm back safely in the green world of the goggles, the surreal, vegetable world of the goggles, softening this mineral kingdom. Gymnastics are not to be advised at this altitude, I'm lying exhausted on the gentle slope of a broad, angled shelf of rising rock. In a moment I'll dead haul my oxygen set up and just breathe the life giving gas for a while.

No soul-force left in me at the present . . . what energy remains is going into warming up and stimulating the circulation in my fingers. Still, as Geoffrey sagely observed: 'A little mystery and silence are rather a good fault in a first man . . . men do not want to be over-enlightened before their turn comes'.

Sandy's up now and I'm just making steps in a steep, icy snow slope, up toward a short and not very promising looking rock wall. A second, bloody gasless pitch if it is to go. It's a long hard way to come to a dead-end . . . I've never had much faith in levitation. The rock face is very badly weathered and in a generally poor state of detrition.

XXI

I've been feeling the tactile temper of the rock . . . the texture of its grain and purchase . . .

A lithological character reading by hand and eye, the weathered rugosity and natural striation, bedding lines smoothed once by sea floor currents . . .

the rhythmic sequence of the sedimentary layers.

Rock is time's most durable weave . . .

This solid rock so saturated and compact in the warp and the quick of the elusive ethereality of time . . . the geological spans in its mineral veins.

Time now set in crystal . . .

The laying down of ages in the strata . . . this inweave of the aeons . . .

Rock gives one the sense of time's true measure.

I finger the touchstone of our brief span.

The chill sense of mortality in the haptic shock from freezing cold stone . . .

And the surface texture of the rocks . . .

that combination of weathering and the composition of the rock . . .

As maybe the physiognomy of a time is the consequence of historical currents, the inexorable, causal nexus of events and the stubborn grain of human character.

Another form of rough tempering.

XXII

There's a suggestive line to the right, but the rock is crumbly and frangible, very unsound, *scabreux de l'escalade* . . . I've a sudden, vivid memory, from early Winchester days, of climbing the ruins of Wolvesey Castle . . . the mouldering wall crumbling under me . . . and a last, desperate leap for my life.

I'm beginning to wish Sandy had painted the oxygen sets with 'Cavorite' that science fiction substance mysteriously opaque to gravity. We could ascend then in the manner of the local saint, Guru Padmasambhava, hitching upon a passing sunbeam. Making ours a second illicit summiting.

But the heavenly conservation of energy! Hail to the Jewel in the Lotus, who could object to coming second to a saint, a man who had reached the summit of ego-annihilation and realised the view.

Only now I'm faced with only one option, this narrow, awkward rock crack, a sheered strain-slip cleavage on the sinistral side in the shadow. And there I have its name, Sinistral Side in the Shadow.

Sheltered here the rock is not freeze-shatter addled. It's not a very long pitch I grant you, but can I do it? That's the question. If it goes I could be up there with Mummery . . . famous for Mallory's Crack, if it doesn't I'll be in the hereafter, with no chance of achieving in old age 'a fine mountain atmosphere of mind'.

O, for the wings of an Avro . . . I don't like this limestone, give me Borrowdale Volcanic or good, rough Skye gabbro. Something you can get a sure grip of . . . the Sphinx was made of limestone . . . my heart's in Chamonix granite, bedded on the fundamental gneiss. It all comes back in the end to the Alps . . . our sublime legacy of orogeny from the Miocene period.

But climbers can't be choosers, especially as I'm about to use Sandy as a ladder, albeit a stout and stalwart human ladder. Yes, it's combined tactics this time, the only way really to tackle it.

Sandy's wearing enough protective, warm clothing, to cushion his flesh from my wing-nails and tricounis.

From Sandy's Atlas shoulders now, the final, testing section of rock-wall. Even with the use of the human ladder it's not within the compass of my reach. It's going to be a tricky crack climb, a large chockstone blocks the exit, a superbly inconvenient feature, everything I could have wished for . . . such a sufficient exiguity of holds.

O, these 'truly delectable places' . . . and our old, dogging familiar . . . *with difficulty* . . . its pregnant moments big as years . . .

The move out, up and around the chockstone should afford a good opportunity to enjoy the circumambient air . . . at its most bracing and spacious. Certainly the crux move of the climb. I've unroped from Sandy just in case, no point in us both going down to the glacier. One sacrifice should suffice for any goddess.

There's only about five feet or so before I can reach a mantelshelf, once I've reached it I'll have a hold and the burr of rock just below should provide a crucial footing.

The trick is to keep the continuity of movement . . . not to get yourself spread-eagled, straddled on the nerve ends of endurance . . . a martyr to the over reach of temptation.

I'll need to use my left knee and forearm, to begin with, for friction holds. Jamming them in the rock crack gently, clenching the muscles to secure the hold, then relieving them lightly to release the pressure, above all no anxious flurry, must keep it nice and steady.

'Friction materially increased by inspiration' and a sustained momentum . . .

I hold my life in balance on the rock, quickened in the agony of this exertion . . . the interminable seconds, wrested out of difficult rock, of painfully long-lived intensity . . .

Eternity is time rendered fully into the present.

XXIII

Shelley is right, we know not what we do not dare . . .

But I almost didn't make it, what an almighty effort . . . that final reach and step out round the chockstone . . . altogether a breezy situation. I'm absolutely bloody exhausted . . . all soul-force spent and winded.

How differently we can experience the current of time in our life, the feel of the pulse of our existence . . . the deep felt sense of being . . . even in the course of a day.

Ordinarily it would have been really quite straightforward, it's not that technically difficult a climb, but at this altitude the climbing becomes exceptionally severe. In the symphony of my imagination this was romantically marked: '*Nobilimente: Alpinismo Acrobatico*'.

The mismatch between the vision I had created in my mind's eye and the bathos of the reality . . . there is a sure-fire droll humour in the canon of incongruity.

But I'm safely on the rock shelf, just trying to get my breath back; feeling very chuffed with myself. The delightful sense of difficulties overcome . . .

This is what one hungers for . . . what the spirit needs, in the face of modern life, is the sense of freedom . . . and that is the essence of the mountains . . . the natural solace of the hills coming with their inspirational air and promise of the heights. And the quickening joy you experience in the feeling of something vast and infinitely serene . . . that mysteriously uplifts the heart and mind . . . and sometimes quietly leads you to an open, very tranquil space . . . beyond the borders of within and without.

XXIV

Sandy's sent my ice axe up, in a clove hitch, on the rope. I'm giving him the thumb's up triumphant. We're in luck, there's a suitable outcrop of rock just ahead round which I can thread the rope as an anchor and then use it to belay and bring up Sandy.

We've done it, we're on for the summit. I should say about two hours away. And then as I checked my watch, I discovered that the crystal was gone and that the minute hand was missing . . . broken in the first, few moves of the climb.

I've gathered from Sandy that it's now 12.57, we could be on the summit by 3 o'clock, which would give us enough time to return . . . but our oxygen isn't going to last much longer, only a short supply of the gas remains. It's impossible to turn back at this stage, Sandy is just as keen to go all out as I am . . . After all, the last two feet of the summit he's expected to take back for Moore's . . . his old House has rather a shortage of cups.

The summit is now only a matter of a snow plod, not a climb, but one of Dr. Johnson's steep walks, a grim slog to the agonised rhythm of the lungs. And it's down to a race with the old Enemy – Time.

Let's see how far our oxygen will take us, then what sort of progress we can make.

It's a pity Sandy's lost his ice axe, when my first oxygen cylinder ran out, just before that first rock step, he'd been taking a photograph, so had carefully put his axe down, then, seeing my difficulties, he came immediately to my aid . . . forgetting his axe.

It'll make things more difficult for him, he's lost his extra hand . . . his pick, support and anchor. Still, it can't be helped . . . the weird of happenstance.

Fortunately the ground now is undemanding . . . we have a clear highway to the summit.

But mist is rolling up the North face dramatically and there are ominous clouds coming up in fat, blossoming flotillas from the Kharta Valley.

The fearful threat of the monsoon . . .

But it isn't that dread host of cloud, massed in heavily, storm-pregnant ranks. With my hard won view from the gods', I can see the horizon clear and calm beyond . . . and blue sky above the summit. That's a good sign . . . the talisman of reassurance.

With luck the mist and clouds might not reach us at this height, otherwise we're in for a squall. A local storm . . . but we'll have the easy terrain in our favour and at altitude the snow falls fine. All now depends on the wind, on the wind not getting up in the Beaufort scale a 'Gorgon's deathly dirge'. Or we'll have to turn back in the teeth of it.

To be resolute in advance as timely to retreat . . .

If only we can remain serenely above the threatening weather . . . Olympian gods for a day.

I can't breathe . . . I can't breathe . . . I'm not getting any oxygen . . .

The desperate, clumsy fumble to remove the mask. I gulp the air as if I'd come up from a dive. Thin, cold air . . . but I can breathe again. The frantic panic of asphyxiation subsides . . . relief breaks in upon me in a heady wave . . .

The inside of my oxygen mask is a Fingal's Cave of ice . . .

I scrunch out the stalactites and stalagmites of saliva and condensation with my gloved thumbs. I rub off some of the lamina of ice from my chin and, after opening the flow valve again on the cylinder, clip my oxygen mask back on. This salvation of oxygen is a mixed blessing.

Sandy's caught up with me and together we trudge on. The pace of our ascent has slowed, the ground is much easier, but the going has got much harder, as in some fairy tale paradox . . .

The three rock steps guarding the summit . . . and each with its own testing ordeal.

XXV

It's time to stop for some tiffin and something to drink . . . just enough to keep body and soul together . . . the old heart up . . . god, I've a Gargantuan thirst . . .

But we can't be long though . . . every minute now is infinitely precious. Which reminds me, I'll take my poor, broken watch off and put it in my pocket. It's seen some service and always been reliable, so I'd like to have it repaired for old time's sake.

Altitude gives one a terribly sweet tooth . . . and even worse . . . an almost insatiable thirst. As it is we're down to our last thermos flask. We must keep something to drink in reserve.

All I can see below now is the eerie ghostliness of mist, the rising wraith-like tops of the menacing clouds . . . we'll soon be enveloped in the chill embrace of all their damnable weather. Still, England expects . . . and I remain sanguine . . . the hobgoblinry of clouds nor the foul fiendishness of weather shall daunt our spirits.

That's it . . . open the flow-valve, clip the oxygen mask on again . . . and we're off, we must be on our way. The great venture . . . and the beckoning prize . . . such a hope to be realised . . . the highest summit of all.

Though the effort required to sustain our sluggish progress is immense. Sandy, that stalwart, broad-shouldered oarsman, and I are labouring . . . labouring mightily.

But Sandy's done so well . . . we've made such a good combination.

Just as a knot is increased in strength by being tied with the lay of the rope, so a good climbing partnership is rendered proof by going with the grain of each character.

We both got our blues for rowing. Sandy's a cracking good oar and rows at No.3. And I used to row at No.7, so we've really been able to discuss all the 27 points of a good stroke. There's a surprising touch of poetry in him too, when he talks of the Cherwell winding through the meadows of Mesopotamia. But he's been hit very hard by Oxford's ignominious defeat, by four and a half lengths this year in the Boat Race. And I'm hoping that today will make it up to him . . . for not having been in the Oxford 'Crock eight' . . . and winning!

Although we've had such fun together . . . the pony race on the Tibetan Plain, stampeding the whole baggage train. The great, black battalions of the yaks lumbering into a thundering gallop . . . the charge of the heavy brigade. Even Jack and Jill, our two, sturdy, mess tent mules took off, bolting under their packed loads.

And the ground shook beneath us, as if Hades himself was coming up to join the party.

I shared Sandy's boyish delight in the discovery of the local merry-go-round, a proto Ferris wheel. The predecessor, he thought, of the big one at Blackpool. How we spun round, looping the loop, the full 360 degrees, leaving our stomachs behind and laughing together. The sacrament of shared fun . . . that's what it's all about . . . the heart of life.

When George Bernard Shaw saw a photograph of us all, on the 1921 Reconnaissance Expedition, he said, 'it looked like a picnic in Connemara surprised by a snowstorm . . . '

Although we looked for all the world a rum crew of desperadoes. The niceties of civilisation are hard to maintain, while in the field and living in a Mummery tent. Shaw more than most should have appreciated that . . . the comically vulnerable thinness of the civilised veneer.

Damn, I'm not getting any oxygen . . . I think this is the end of the cylinder . . . I'm just checking to see that my mask hasn't iced up again. No, it's the end of the 'English air' . . . no more oxygen.

Time to disencumber myself of the apparatus, it's all down now to red corpuscles and the capacity of the lungs. Momentarily, I feel as light as air . . . released from all the weight of gravity . . . and now I experience the full leadenness of my body in the effort to step upwards . . . without the inspiration of the 'English air'. All now is Herculean labour . . . between the hard and heavy breathing-times of laboured panting rest.

The fabled goddess exacts her toll . . . the sacred will have its sacrificial rite from the profane. The eternal order of things is not mocked.

Filigree petals . . . graven of crystal . . . blossoming out of the wind . . .

The silent crystallogenesis of snow . . . and all is coldly into white transforming, a world of swirling flakes, cadenced in the wind . . . a world without horizon. The heartening prospect of the summit is gone, we're left only with a featureless, grim Sisyphean plod, shrouded in powdery flurries of thin, fine snow . . . a mirror fugue of all my worst fears and anxieties.

Mountains have their own perversity . . .

I'm already drolly festive, sequinned with snow . . . like a Pearly King . . . and we can only move this slowly now . . . as if we were slowly turning into snowmen . . . to fit into the still immobility of the mountainside.

Well, who would true valour see . . . let him come hither. We're experiencing to the full degree Dr. Kellas's dissociation curve of oxyhaemoglobin in the blood . . . it steepens ever increasingly above 25,000ft. 'The climber near the summit of Mt. Everest will probably be on his last reserves in the way of acclimatisation and strength'.

This immense strain on the heart . . . and the desperate labour of the lungs! Dr. Kellas's curve . . . is the measure of a Promethean endurance test.

Thank god, the wind's not got all its teeth in . . .

From what I could tell of the signs, this storm looked as if it would blow out fairly quickly, if it doesn't . . . we'll have to turn back . . .

We're both feeling the bitter cold, though Sandy assures me, Spitzbergen was even worse.

But looking at his face, I can see clearly the strain of our brutally, cruel labour.

The struggle to breathe . . . in this suffocatingly thin air . . . God, I'm beginning to feel like some poor insect in a killing jar . . . that's what this great spire peak is . . . a tantalising killing cone for trespassing mortals in their hubris . . . a deathly horrible zone.

At least the cold prevents the snow from getting sticky, but fresh snowfall will slow the going on the summit snowfield . . . and all the while it's making our descent more treacherous.

The frost-riven shards of dark, grey shale strewn and littered on the steeply angled ground and this bitter wind, driving the icy snow into our faces, reminds me of the march across the gravel plain on the Tibetan Plateau, that made even the Llanberis Pass look like a green and pleasant land, 'the very abomination of desolation' in Norton's description. It was to Sandy's mind as barren as the surface of the moon, but it reminded me of the wasted landscape that Childe Roland must journey through, 'grey plain all round & rubble, sand & stark black dearth'.

Curious that now approaching the summit the ground, once again, reminds me of the *Dark Tower*. I once thought that the passionate pilgrim was a hero . . . as if the sources of human motivation were that simple.

The process of ageing can afford us sobering views into our inscape . . . the painful insights in which the pearls of some wisdom may form.

We are only managing a slow, punishing progress, the agonising ascent of winded octogenarians. Seven paces then we stop and gasp for breath. We'll carry on till four before making any decisions . . . that'll still give us enough time to ensure a safe return.

We're passing the final marker, the weathered, old guard to the inner sanctum. And fortunately it's no *gendarme* but only an addled, crazed outcrop of buckled-up rock, which we can walk round below. The last rock step, before the start of the summit snowfield. It doesn't compare with the rock splinters of Castell-y-Gwynt . . . the Castle of the Winds.

Sandy's gasping out: "Barnes . . . the final stretch . . . of the course!"

XXVI

The summit vault looms above us now, a coldly bewitching siren, and so heart-breakingly close, only the syllables of time run mockingly down against us . . . the beginning of the avalanche of disappointment . . . as our bodies begin to feel more aged and decrepit. I rub the hoary beard of crusted ice on my chin, all spangled with snow and with my present, doddering pace, I'm like some bumbling, senescent Abominable Snowman . . . or old King Lear come to reason with the elements . . . a pantaloon . . . and this is a young man's war.

From the top of the second rock step, the summit looked so close, it didn't look anything like this distance away . . . what a potent illusion . . . probably a cruelly seductive freak of the arid, thin air . . . and I'm beginning to think now, that we'll have to turn back before Mortlake. The shattering disappointment not to make the finishing line . . . to forgo the crown of success after all we've been through.

But strangely, that awful prospect leaves me oddly indifferent, as if I'm beyond caring either way . . . being numbed in some deep, psychic anaesthesia . . . utterly becalmed in the doldrums of insouciance . . . bereft of all the passion of purpose . . .

Weather and time are against us now in the end . . . I've always said that we would need a constant spirit of kindness from the mountain itself if we were to succeed . . .

The prize is so tantalisingly *there* for the taking, only we have not time enough nor strength to combat the weather, as well as the oxygen starved air. We gave it our best whack . . . to turn our backs forlornly on our hope . . . The resolution to return, not to molest her ancient, solitary reign.

But wait . . . wait . . . Heavens be praised! The weather is changing . . . it's changing in our favour, the snowfall's thinning out . . . and the wind . . . the wind is dying down now to a sough, as if the sky was running out of breath like us . . . and it too expires in an unearthly shade of blue. Sublime, that's the word. . . . and it's our luck . . .

Through the last sky-fluttering flakes of snow, lightly spindling in the sunlight now, the pyramid spire of the summit shines, resplendent as the great pyramid of Cheops once did, in the gone time of the Pharaohs: a transcendent dais of some absconding god . . . the shimmering absence . . . and the deadly cold.

How can I turn back now from this vision? The great hope and expectation of so many years . . . all the prize and glory of the skyward reaching soar of it on high . . .

It is the sunlit answer to my prayer, seen through protecting stained glass, the peerless peak, filtered an unearthly shade of green, through the shield of my snow goggles. Man is not a creature of this light.

I'm looking at Sandy, questioningly with my eyes; his face is set in determination. He grins and nods back, without a word . . . and everything is understood between us.

This is our magnificent chance . . . a prodigious gamble . . . we're going to go all out . . . push our luck to the limit . . . there doesn't really seem to be a choice . . . we're like punch-drunk fighters . . . held only in the unreasoning, dead grip of rigidly fixated purpose . . . drawn on inexorably . . . blind to everything but the victory beckoning now before us . . . Completely in thrall to that captivating promise . . . We can't give up . . . the unequal contest . . . our slogging match . . . with this mad, glorious opportunity and only . . .

The moliminous effort to breathe the meagre air . . .
Let not common sense mock this useless toil

Trying to prove the need for oxygen a heresy, is now a very slow torture by ordeal. The hard, empiric way to establish an upper bound to human possibility. Youth in its proud, idealistic folly . . . god . . .

Had I become reconciled to compromise, that fudged hallmark of maturing years. How one's mettle is muddied by life . . . some things are too painful for words.

If only I had gone for the full load . . . with all three bottles on the sets. This wisdom of hindsight comes . . . more overwhelming than the view, with all its additional, wasting burden . . . the nagging self-reproach and the bitter regret . . . the leaden crown of being so fatuously wise after the event.

Now as I huff and puff for air . . . god, for that third bottle left to spare. 'If only' is the midwife of most tragedies . . . but history can make heroes out of fools, especially if their luck holds out. Success is such an artful alchemy . . . it even obscures the uncanny covenant between fate and irony.

I will complain, yet praise . . .

Just a short, steep climb up the summit snow-cap . . .

Almost snail-slow . . . our stop and go, halt ascension . . . stumbling down on our knees . . . exhausted . . . in an agony of panting . . . to struggle back up . . . unsteady against the odds . . . our resolve just braced by the sure hope of the summit . . . The gruelling effort now put into making a step . . . the grim toll of it . . . god . . . each step upward now as penitential as a Station of the Cross . . . God . . .

Onwards and heavenward . . . hellishly heavenward to . . .

God, only rest . . . heavenly rest . . . rest for breath . . . god . . . Everest . . .

One last, crippling effort . . . Christ . . .

A final, agonising 'red grind' . . .

XXVII

God . . . the King of Heights . . . where aspirations end . . . the heart's sublime content . . . its own reward . . . nothing more this side of heaven . . . all the realisation of the dream . . . the place of fame and elegy . . . Peak XV . . . the abode of Deity . . .

And where is the place of understanding?

The chance of a lifetime . . . god . . .

To meet the sun upon the summit . . .

In the melting mood . . .

The Kingdom Come . . .
The light more glorious . . .
Tears standing in the eyes . . .

'BRITISHERS' GREAT ADVENTURE . . .'

To be nearer heaven . . . god . . .
the kingdom of the Saints of Light . . .
will elevate the human spirit . . .
a crowning feat of clay.

The highest endeavour . . .
what boots it, god . . . to scale the heights,
to launch our challenge to the stars,
to dare the generations . . .
to be far famed . . . to wear the crown
watery eyed in the plaintful wind . . .

a fugitive king of empyrean space.

But where shall wisdom be found *in excelsis* . . .

Peck's Hardening Lotion for the feet . . .
to cushion the 'spirit of adventure'.

Almost a god's eye view . . . the chantry of the winds . . .
The 'Third Pole' finally conquered . . .
queered the pitch for posterity . . .

But 'fulfilled the destiny . . .
to struggle and to understand . . .'

The effort to realise the view . . .
god, such a bloody struggle . . .

O, the scintillant play of the light . . .

I look down now on bright, white cumulus clouds . . .
soft with all the pathos of the transience of things . . .

I could weep . . . for joy . . .

Unearthly sunlight irradiates this world . . .
as if it would transilluminate the soul . . .

The incandescent inbeing of our star . . .
the lucent universe of light around . . .

The only shadows here are ones we bring ourselves.

All the racking toil and sweat . . . the doubts and anguish, the heartache and the bitter disappointments of the setbacks on the way . . . are so inextricably made up now into the experience of this moment. It's the mysterious depths of our inscape that imbue the landscape with its deepest, living hues.

A world of sunlit, snowy mountain peaks . . . a phantasmogoric, petrographic province . . . the 'seat of the snows' . . . the Great Himalaya from end to end . . . the wild, high solitudes serene above the region cloud.

'Have we conquered an enemy . . . none but ourselves . . .'
A terrible, Pyrrhic victory and the reckoning is not paid.

Great climbers have been caught . . . on the knees of the gods . . . sometimes again andante . . . always be a slight chance of disaster.

Sandy, wide-eyed and breathless now, in the heaven-born moment . . . a painfully panting figure standing in the sun, so crowned with happiness and in a dreadful state. We bloody did it. We made it. Enchanted ground . . .

We came as pilgrims . . . a 'parfit glorious pilgrymage' . . .

And as the Abrahams observed of the Great Gully Climb on Craig yr Ysfa . . . 'a lengthy expedition of exceptional severity'.

A spectacular *tour d'horizon* . . . a pity I couldn't give to rapture all my shivering bones.

Trailing high clouds rent by the glory of its sovereign, snow-capped peaks . . . the crowning orogenic belt in the world . . . where the light-minded wind alone rules all supreme . . .

This stupendous, geomorphological panorama . . . a sanctuary of wildness, with its numinous sense of the transcendent . . . its cast of the Eternal. . . . a haven for the spirit . . .

I'm looking down into the great cirque, the lunar stillness of its snow basin, a coruscating sea of frozen tranquillity. I feel as if I could just walk miraculously on this theophany of sunlight over to Nuptse . . . my body transubstantial . . . an airy tabernacle completely leavened and billowy with all my light-headedness . . . drunk on this brilliantly intoxicating lift of light.

I must consult . . . god . . . consult the oracle . . . the astrolabe . . . God, I mean my pocket altimeter . . . just as well I've read my Whymper . . . Chaucer wrote about the astrolabe . . .

Must see exactly what it reads . . . my Chaucer . . . the astrolabe . . . my specially made altimeter, god . . . was made for the occasion . . . a precision *vade mecum* . . . calibrated for up to 30,000 ft.

Comforting to know the exact altitude before you step off the world . . . something to do with science . . . my own vanity and curiosity. At least I don't have to sight it.

And the height by altimeter is . . . 27,630ft . . . 27,630ft . . . and even after giving it a shake . . . still disappointingly a reading . . . a truncated reading of 27, 630ft . . . which leaves only . . . leaves . . . god . . . leaves only . . . god . . . leaves only 1,372ft missing.

Exasperated, I tap the glass face sharply . . . and it just falls out . . . God, I'm lost for an adequate expletive . . . and can only stare at it dumbly now in consternation and disbelief . . . I can't see the crystal of the blasted altimeter anywhere in the snow around my feet . . . Damn it all, it's just not my bloody day for contributing to science . . . the exact height of Everest remains a mystery. The goddess keeps some of her mystique. That's the bugger of divinity for you.

Sandy is struggling to set up the camera, pulling out the bellows, one for the Mt. Everest Committee, a breathtaking shot of Makalu. The proof is in the negative . . . so to speak . . . the photographic evidence . . . an advertisement for the Kodak Vestpocket, autographic camera . . .

I won't smile for the uncertain promise of posterity . . . its indifference is too much with us.

Poor, bloody Sandy, it's a deuce of an awkward, fiddly business trying to set the correct aperture, with clumsy, mittened hands and painfully, brittly cold fingers.

Having shoved his pith helmet back, he's kneeling on the summit cone, peering down into the little prism of the viewfinder, a painstaking supplicant for the art.

Let's hope the cantankerous Hinks, Sir Francis and all the gaggling Committee are suitably appreciative.

Something historic for them to frame, another trophy to hang on the Club wall . . .

Pink to Peak XV: Old Union Jack on the summit.

With my back to the wind, I reach inside, underneath all my layers of warm clothing, for the cherished photograph of Ruth, which I had so carefully wrapped inside my favourite dress handkerchief, together with the bundle of her letters, taking them out as carefully as sacred relics.

The high altitude wind suddenly catches and snatches them from my hand . . . my hopeless fingers almost stalactites . . . in an agony of pathetic fumbling . . .

And I can only watch helplessly as they tear away . . . all her precious letters . . . her love . . .

I haven't even the breath to cry out . . .

As I turn in to face the harshness of the wind . . . desperately trying to save the photograph.

I'd promised myself, long ago, that if I ever reached the summit, I would bury a photograph of Ruth on the top, as a symbol of my love; honouring her as the inspiration, the spirit enabling me to succeed. And perhaps even as a propitiation for the hubris of such a violation.

Hacking out a space with my ice axe in the summits icy, snow pack; the effort is almost too much. Clumsily interring her image was not at all as I had imagined. The grim, desultory manner of it, a perfunctory business, neither time nor spirit for any ceremony . . . and all the while the raving wind . . . the bone-numbing cold.

The poignant shards of the dream stark against the sub-zero reality . . .

We must leave this godforsaken heaven to the lamentations of the wind, keening their oracles of death sheer in the scales of minus zero.

Time we were gone. We've got to start going down or we'll be here until eternity yawns. I must remember though to pick up a small specimen of loose rock from near the summit . . . a pocket-piece . . . for a keepsake . . . something to show the geologists . . . a memento of Everest.

God, it's going to be a hopeless race . . . we have now so little time . . . less than two hours of daylight left . . . the impossible race against the eventide . . . and benighting has begun. We've only a prayer . . .

A prayer in hell's chance . . . and to think of what we've achieved.

The first, few minutes of the descent are always the most unnerving . . . the eye beholds a giddying panorama, the vertiginous falling away beneath the feet . . . it takes time to adjust for even the most seasoned climber.

The extra demand on already tired nerves, the sudden awareness of near exhaustion, and the enormous, daunting task before us: 'the last giddy hours of dread endurance' . . . the inner struggle not to be overwhelmed. And I've got to keep my part up even more.

Age and experience be what succour . . .

But rigour now has gone to bed . . .we have no margin left . . . only our trust in luck and the mountain's kindness . . . And the inevitably less attentive, weary time of the descent . . . provides the ripest hour for accidents . . . when the mind no longer has its keen focus . . . fatigue and tiredness exacting all their debilitating toll on the body and mind.

Bloody hell . . . god, we're going to be benighted.

The powdery snow sloughs up, scattering-bright in front of our boots . . . slowing our glissade in its soft, downy drag.

Canting the feet and swinging the weight of the body . . . trying to reduce friction and increase pace . . . all is now a desperate attempt to make up precious time . . . as we ski and skate with the soles of our boots . . . glissading down the summit snowfield . . . ploughing down . . . through glistening troughs . . . and furrowed glittery runs . . . trailing small cascades . . . in the play of the light . . . the radiant shimmer of it all . . . sparkling and glinting . . . in the blaze and glare of the brilliant sunlight . . . that catches all the exhilarating glory of the clouds below . . . some playground of the gods . . . only I'm at the ready with my ice axe . . . we're roped up as Sandy is without his . . . I'm the brake and anchor man . . . should we fall and start to careen out of control . . . picking up an avalanche momentum . . . toward a wild and final career down to the glacier.

But I've such a weird sense of mental flatness . . . no excitement or exhilaration . . . just a sort of numbness . . . as if I could just sit down to the wildest wailing of the wind . . . and set quietly into an insensible, crystal frigidity. Lord, I must think of Ruth . . . the warm heart-hold of her love . . . my promise . . . mustn't lose sight of her . . . she's depending on me . . . the children . . . our future . . . all our hopes . . .

XXVIII

Knowing one's common sense and judgement to be fuddled by the effects of altitude provides no effectual protection, the mind moves only as it can . . . dimly along its impaired pathways. Out of its element and halt, it loses its immediate cohesion.

The irony of it is we're in a paradisaic world of iridescent sunshine under a beatific, blue sky: an awe-inspiring paradise of Avalokiteshvara. It makes the desperateness of our situation feel unreal . . . bathed in this heavenly beatitude.

A nightmare flight out of heaven . . . as if we were angels on fire seeking now for the mercy of oblivion . . . the cold comfort of the unforgiven.

We too were stars of the morning . . . exhausted now we must plummet . . .

Ex paradiso . . . in purgatorio . . .

Shadows but of ourselves . . .

The pale revenants of the achievement of the day . . . as ones who once had wings . . .

And with the inevitable relaxation of purpose . . . the dangerous enervation coming in the aftermath of triumph . . . the slackening off of psychic tonus . . . such a struggle now to keep alive the vital alertness of the mind.

The insidious glozing of success . . . can be as deadly as the glazing of black ice.

I'm determined not to end up like bloody, heroic Scott. You can keep the sad votaries of the cult of the hero . . . the deceiving aura of the romantic halo . . . I still thirst for 'the maddening wine of life'. Give me the living, frail flaws of flesh and blood . . . my creaturely suit of the muddy vesture . . . our common, prelapsarian stuff so prone . . . to frostbite. Better frostbitten than illustriously stuffed . . . a lifeless piece of worthy taxidermy . . . embalmed in legend . . . a thing of ghastly glory in some poet's deathless tale.

But it's otherworldly enough now for any damn saga . . . and all romantically mantled, witchingly sabled in treacherous snow . . . only the wind is no longer wracked by its restless rune.

If only I hadn't broken my bloody watch . . . god, there's always time for regret.

At last, the first salient of our retreat . . . that indifferent sentinel, the third rock step . . . Doubting Castle. One last look back at the summit now, almost engrailed in the fresh snow, catching the first blush of the Alpenglow, turning gold in the radiant alchemy of the sun; the goddess in the full panoply of her pageant, sublimely reasserting her serene remoteness.

That's it, I'll not look back again . . . too little daylight time left to waste on siren majesty. I'm free . . . free of the fascination of supernal heights.

A time of absolution from ambition . . . where only life and death are at issue.

XXIX

Sandy's finding it hard, but he's keeping up. We've got to get back down the second rock step while there's still light enough for the task. It's only bloody dogged as does it now . . .

We must keep up this gruelling momentum . . . to have any hope in hell.

I seem to be looking at my body from the outside, curiously detached . . . the locus of my consciousness displaced . . . a strangely disembodied observer.

How beautiful on the mountain are the feet of him that brings good tidings . . .

The white monotony of the snow turns dazzling chameleon in the late sun . . . radiantly taking on a celestial coat of coruscating fire.

A paean of wild, elemental beauty . . . the transfiguration of a landscape . . . a resplendent transmutation in a glaze of all the lustrous lambency of the light.

My wearied, all too mortal steps, in flat discord to the tonal mood . . . making a pathetic, jarring counterpoint . . .

And the snow is now a seeming golden lava . . .

How I stumble through this awesome scenic hallowing . . . where an angel would be wonder-struck and lost in marvelling . . . pressing on stone-cold, mindless to all its sublime and aureate glory.

My lengthening shadow stalks me, stark and looming darkly . . .
a grotesque, mocking giant in this kingdom of effulgence . . .

I feel so tremendously, pathetically insignificant . . . it's quite gone to my head . . . my shattering inconsequentiality here . . . and such an unnerving, dizzying sense of being unreal . . . the annihilating laughter of the gods . . . and that all unsteadying, heavy wave of tiredness . . . the first, threatening undertow of exhaustion.

The difficulty is to just keep going . . . when you lose the immediate sense of urgency . . . that hold of your grip . . . that's when it gets dangerous . . . and death can come as softly out of the cold as a dream.

I've the uncanny sense of another . . . an ethereal presence, some nervous hallucination, a good angel or a fetch? An Alpine *Doppelgänger*, perhaps it's the ghost of Almer come to be my guide, my Virgil in this purgatory.

The mind has mountains . . . its dreams of aspiration and 'cliffs of fall frightful, sheer' . . . with whelming moods that can fearfully conjure. *Ach du lieber*! Let it be old Almer, *der besten Führer einer.*

One's good angel should have only the best *bona fides* . . .

How far below and small Changtse looks, the last of day and the coming night held in balance on the scales of its summit, the triangular east face of its pyramid casting an ominously umbrageous warning . . . the dreadful tidings of that lengthening shadow.

So infinitely precious now is this last arc of sunlight . . . the waning glow of its fraying radiance . . . the quietening, pensive air of last things . . . the shiver of mortality . . . the haunting hour of metaphysics that sombrely attends the pathos of the dying sun.

God, I'm coughing fit to wrench my guts out . . .

XXX

We're coming back to our weathered, anchor rock, round which we must rope ourselves down the rock wall, on the double rope. The tricky part is running off the rope after. It's a case of getting Sandy lowered down, securely to the snow slope below. Then I follow him down on the rope, with his help and guiding arms if necessary. No easy feat for tired, exhausted men, who feel a more gravid law of gravity.

Sandy's clambering over the edge of the mantelshelf of rock, roping-down, leaving me waiting anxiously for his signal on the rope.

I'm lowering myself down now, to Sandy and to safely planted boots in snow. I stand relieved and breathless in exhaustion, just as the bloody light begins to go . . . But I can't move just yet . . . must get my breath back.

We've got to run the rope off the rock first, keeping it coming smoothly and continuously, then, to prevent the last, few feet snagging, we both pull together on the rope, in one even movement, to give it a springing release.

It hurtles down thumping Sandy's pith helmet . . . God, I'd forgotten to warn him to mind his head. Hard to remember everything . . . when it's difficult to remember anything.

Heeling our boots in cautiously, we carefully descend down the tricky snow slope to the rock ledge, carefully balancing on our scraping Alpine nails to the start of our diagonal, descent climb.

It's going to be an extremely difficult business, there's nowhere for any secure belay stance . . . and though the recent snow gives us a wan light, it makes the going all the more treacherous.

I've got to patiently coach and shepherd Sandy down now, trusting the rope will act as a sufficient 'psychological belay' to give him enough of a sense of security.

But climbing down is tricky at the best of times . . . a more awkward art . . . less certain and familiar . . . it requires real practice . . . the necessary physical movements involved are more trying and exacting to execute . . . the eye has to select holds from some fiendishly unaccustomed angles . . . And here, god, help us, we must somehow mole our way in the murk.

We're climbing down very slowly, making sure of handholds first, before allowing the feet to divine the way . . . test out footholds and lead. I've told Sandy to cleave fast to salvation by faithfully following the holy trinity . . . never less than three extremities should have a hold on the rock at any one time . . .

Sandy's doing well, but the extreme fatigue is telling . . .

Using the fingers and the heels of the hands, groping cautiously with the feet for footholds . . . struggling awkwardly with my clumsy boots to read the rock like Braille.

This adagio: *In Memoriam Cantabrigiensis* . . . the challenge of the college roof after dark. An education can stand a man in good stead.

But I have to admit the strain is almost overwhelming, that last, heavy scrabble down the rock wasn't good. The bluntness of painfully frozen fingers on frigid rock . . .

And the clumsiness of tiredness now is lethal . . . every minute the odds stack up against us.

One final, awkwardly tricky section of rock, I'm leaning back, ice axe wedged in a crack to effect a sort of anchor hold, while Sandy descends the last slab of rock.

There's only an ice axe and a heart-felt prayer between us and the glooming glacier below. Thank the Lord . . . he's made it safely, it's my turn now to climb down to . . . a final slither between Sandy and the rock . . . thank god for Sandy.

The enormous heady tide of relief . . . I can't believe our luck still . . . we've bloody done it, the grim obstacle is behind us. And there's no frantic need to hurry anymore, the worst has happened . . . we're benighted. The awful, eerie calm now in the eye of disaster.

XXXI

Only a few, pale stars coldly choir the deepening shades of gloom, the primeval mystery of the darkening hush of night . . . when the crystal silence of the snow alone holds its frosty communion with the stars . . . inimical to life through the cold, life-less reign of the dark . . .

Time's first occult haven . . . and our immemorial bogey-man.

You can hear the frostbiting cold, scrunching down hard into the snow . . .

feel the ache of it, through the pinched flesh of the body, as it gnaws at the bones.

Our benighted remoteness now from friends . . . companions . . . loved ones and all the homely, peopled world . . . we might as well be on the Moon. And for the life of me, I must somehow keep in a miraculous vein of bloody obdurate hope.

Against the dark, I'll light my candle lantern, strike the match to kindle the flame of our primal amity with fire, its warm and sanctuary light . . . the radiant comforter of fears.

We can rest now and enjoy a bit of tiffin, eat some prunes and the last of the Mintcake, chumble a few raisins and take stock. But god, I'd really love some hot tea . . . just gallons . . . gallons of hot, sweet tea.

Perhaps a snow-pear will provide some comfort. First make your snow-pear . . . then suck it and see.

I'm trying to make a snow-pear, but the snow is too powdery and cold to gel, it dissolves in my gloves like dust . . . dust and ashes. I feel like a small child that's lost its ice cream . . . or as one of Keats's ancient Titans . . . a bemused sense that the glory has departed. What authority do I have now in this jeopardy? And as those Titan has-beens – I too feel superannuated . . . and alarmed by the sense of my own strengthlessness.

I try again, risking bare fingers to warm the snow sufficiently for it to compact. I manage to form a small, ill-shaped lump; my fingers now are agony. I suck my icy pear for cold comfort, a monarch of sheer misery.

I've never cared for the taste of snow, its peculiar mineral taste . . . I can see Sandy now, in the light of his torch, as happy as a man with a snow-pear.

While there's life . . . there's complaining . . . in the beginning was the discontent . . . harbouring the complaint . . . the first, heartfelt refrain . . . our companion *leitmotif*.

Well, I shan't need my snow goggles anymore . . . I'll take them off and stow them away in my pocket for safekeeping. It's carrots, they say, help you see in the dark . . . my kingdom for a carrot . . . that's the whirligig of time for you . . . God, the poignant irony of its revenges.

We can't go on much longer at this level, we're coming to the end of our reserves, with all the trial still to come of the difficult traverse back to the first rock step, in this abysmal light. And the pitch will be in an even more difficult and treacherous condition with the fresh snowfall.

I've got to find another way . . . some blasted easier route.

There's a snow terrace lower down, its cushioning of snow shows it up more clearly in relief in this light . . . if we could get down to it before we're overwhelmed by sheer exhaustion, we might still have a slight chance. Just a case of shuffling along it . . . that'll be the limit of our capacity . . . should get us more or less back to our Camp. We're not in a position now to choose our line of retreat.

To find a route down the mountainside, taking the lines of least resistance, to the comparative safety of the terrace. Lead kindly rock . . . we'd be so damn lucky . . . and on these confounded, crazed, declivitous slabs . . . Anyhow, let' s try to lose height as quickly as possible . . . it should help to ease our physical condition . . . make the business of breathing a little easier. Wishful thinking perhaps . . . but it's a poor sort of hope that can't envision triumphing over experience.

We mustn't lose all heart . . . in spite of the cold, even if the spirit now has shrunk within us. 'In great climbing, as in warfare, morale is the dominating factor'.

I can tell you old Pindar was wise . . . good fortune really is the best prize. If we can only just get back to the tent . . . melt some snow for a brew up, crawl inside our sleeping bags . . . conjure up warmth into our bodies snugly cocooned in answered prayers.

This cold has a deathly, skeletal hold . . . we must get going and keep moving . . .

We'll stay roped up from now on, even if the ground did not demand it, a be-nighted party does best to rope up. The communion of the rope is for protection, psychological as much as physical . . . it is our 'psychic' link. But it requires careful managing . . . it mustn't be allowed to 'feint in coils' . . .

We have moonlight and coldly indifferent stars . . . Sandy's torch and my candle-lantern . . . together we pick out a groping, nocturne way . . . fatigue to the counterpoint of necessity. All that's missing is Dr. Hingston asking us to blow mercury up a tube and do some jolly, long division.

Mercifully the patrolling wind has gone mysteriously to slumber with the demons . . . leaving the mountain quiet as a dream . . . an uncanny, otherworldly stillness . . . in which my strained and laboured breathing only provides a pained and hoarse accompaniment.

The power to keep going when you feel no energy, but just utter exhaustion . . . it all comes down to this in the end . . . you either make an agony of effort . . . and find a desperate salvation . . . or you've had it.

And salvation . . . salvation is bloody buggering . . .

XXXII

My mysterious, phantasmal companion is back with me again . . . more vividly real and present . . . a ghostly apparition . . . some hallucination of my oxygen starved brain . . . or a symptom of my nervous exhaustion . . . like the 'angels' or Gemini of the battlefield . . . the Angel of Mons . . . the Comrade in White.

It's crazy but I'm sure it's Rupert . . . Rupert Brooke to the life . . . as he was that day on the Cam . . . such a haunting figure becomes a ghost best . . . the mournful phantom of our age . . . forever young in death . . . sad icon now of our lost generation . . . full of the unfulfilled promise of youth . . . the cherished personification of so much awful loss . . . that lost bright spirit of happier days . . . of the summer before our time came of age.

Odd that he's come to harp and carp along with me . . .
he wasn't a very good Mephistopheles in our play
and I'll have none of his songs of pilgrims unreturning.

But at least I'll be able to match Collie's spooky tale now, which at the time seemed such a load of hooey . . . about those eldritch footsteps on misty Ben MacDhui.

After a degree of exposure on Everest, you can see the shades of the dead, something to do with the atmospherics . . . and the rarefied air acting like the smoke for the Python's inspiration . . . the amphibological speak of the oracle.

If I should die . . . think only . . . some snowy terrace of a foreign mountain . . . forever England . . . I must get back . . . back to England . . . Yes, back to England . . . for the gentle rain . . . the dull, grey heavens . . . the land of such dear souls . . . little kindly winds . . . flowers to love . . . and hills so green in memory . . . the gently undulating Gogs . . . Mam Tor . . . the fantastic hills of the Chankly Bore . . . the lyric traverse of the Malverns . . . poetry of which cherished memories are made.

And will the railway still be running
up to the top of Mt. Snowdon for tea . . .

God, the luxury of heresy and sacrilege . . .
only the view is never realised as it should be.

But after this, I'll not have to see the ugly snout of the East Rongbuk Glacier ever again. How I've come to dread that dragging *via dolorosa* of the long march in.

I must concentrate on footings . . . balance, the great weary task of getting down. 'My strength is not the strength of stones.' I've such a leaden tiredness in my bones. Sluggishness oozes through my veins . . . the aching slow, shivery-coldness of my body . . . I could just collapse into this painfully dragging fatigue . . . fall into its gravitational well . . . succumbing to my overwhelming weariness . . . and lie down in its promise of the sleep . . . sleep of utter exhaustion . . . the comfort of oblivion . . . how seductive . . . only a freezing death would crystallise in me . . . and ice its vacant, grisly smile upon my face.

This is hell, sheer hell . . . and in this infernal light . . .

Happy are the long suffering . . . when they have no choice. I couldn't choose a prosaic happiness . . . an English heaven. Sod it . . .

I know a glacier where fretted penitentes flare
And crevasses yawn in a world of ultra violet glare

Where sunny caves of ice, deep aquamarine, shiver lambently in scintillant iridescence; the intensity of it in the high altitude, hyaline air, more unearthly and oneiric than stately Xanadu.

All that rucked and buckled up ice, a frozen charivari; like the Charge of the Light Brigade . . .

Half a metre, half a metre, half a metre onward,
out of the glaciated valley, shatter'd and sunder'd,
tumbled and reared the ice-flow . . .

Great thoughts by England given . . .
no time now to look for fossils . . .

Molluscs have never been found . . .
so pick up any snail shells . . .

no trifle unconsidered . . .
the last infirmity of a noble mind.

I want to creep inside my shell . . .

Withdraw into my bones . . .
castle myself in the warmth
of the innermost bastion,
the safe marrow of my body.

And to think that I once had a brain,
a mind that was quick-conceiving.

O, God our help in ages past . . .

Must keep the single eye of the mountaineer. Let the paths of glory lead only to my sleeping bag. *Requiescat in pace* molluscs everywhere. *Dulce et decorum est pro patria dormire* . . . that's what I always say . . . I'll sleep more lifelessly than the dead.

God, give me oxygen and strength.

I move so slowly to the agonised beat of my lungs. These great, sloping tiles of rock may look easy, but they're damn tricky. One slip and you could be at the bottom awfully dead, but not so bloody tired.

I have an instinctual feel for rock, a natural style: a real poet's touch. Only the memory of it now . . . and the baffled feel of not to feel it.

I rest and pant for oxygen like an old man, trembling weak with cold and exhaustion: a poor, pathetic creature out of its element. I feel an almost geological age, a living fossil; a perfect specimen for the Alpine Club . . . 'a club for gentlemen who happen to climb'.

This is worse than the potato race on board the ship coming out. It was Sandy who talked me into it . . . I almost won . . . but for that last potato . . . the last potato really was impossible.

If I get down alive, I'll hang my ice axe up . . . I'll make a pilgrimage to Stoke Poges and give to sadness all I have . . .

In my old age, I'll go south in winter, following instinctive, migrating birds trued to the warm beat of the sun.

You can keep peaks, passes and glaciers . . .

I can understand Rupert's *heimweh* for the South Seas . . . the tropic sway, a *NoaNoa* land of sun-ripe colours, exotic flowers, the stippling shade of palms, warm surf spumescent between the toes, the radiant warmth of the wildering sand . . .

I must go down to the seas again . . .
get back to Albion's pebbly shores.

Pity Rupert hasn't got a chota peg of mummia . . . a shot of brandy cheered us all up wonderfully in '22 . . .

O, for a piping hot mug of 'Mummery's Blood' . . . some of Epps's *'grateful comforting'* cocoa . . . or even a noggin of yaks blood with the Yetis. Unless our mysterious Abominable Snowmen are as coldly indifferent as the Torquay audience . . .

'The English coldness is so overwhelming . . . '

Perhaps our remote, rude cousins the Yetis, with their great ophthalmic eaves, will be enchanted into coyness by the delicate brow-ridge of *Homo Sapiens*.

We'll sense a mutual kinship, the unconscious memories of our shared arboreal past. Climbers speak the same language everywhere . . . the last gift of the nursery of the tree canopy.

XXXIII

Now the moon has gone . . . we're left like lost souls in Stygian gloom. And I'm losing the sense of being effectively present . . . the wasting erosion of my enervated will . . . thinking ghosts out into nothingness . . . the vacant climate of my mind . . . this wasted inscape penetrated occasionally . . . by remote, deadened feelings . . . the body's desperate autonomic promptings . . . the dulled clamour of the animal instinct for life.

I feel as if I had to rise from the grave . . . only I lack the motive power to do so . . . the sufficient breath of life.

Near freezing in the dark . . . still trying cautiously to test out holds and footings in the barely visible rock . . . I move in coldness like a ghost . . .

Just this bare, animating instinct in me, pared down to the last nerve dendrites. But as Geoffrey wrote in *Mountain Craft*, our definitive pandect of modern climbing, 'to sit down is an all too vulgar error . . .'

I can see it now before my eyes, monumental in bronze, myself in effigy, larger than life. Oh, dear god, a Gulliver Size! With indomitable mien upon my chiselled face, the very lineaments of courage *in extremis*, artistically cast, triumphant in climbing boots, in an heroic pose, ice axe manfully brandished on a subdued lump representing Everest conquered . . . beaten into submission by the noble spirit of man.

Oh, bring me my cap and bells . . . by heavens! Pigeons will have the convenience of me.

A Man-Mountain must have his spoils . . .

So much then for Captain Pride . . . in Kensington Gardens with Speke and Peter Pan.

When I consider how my light is spent . . . but I'll be famous . . . appearing on cigarette cards in a series of famous sporting types . . . and immortalised in a cartoon in Punch.

My boots will be painted by William Nicholson . . . to be set beside those of Gertrude Jekyll . . . two sweated in symbols of human endeavour.

How I miss the garden at the Holt . . . the earthy itch of green fingers . . . that pungent, intimate smell of soil.

I have been so great a . . . so great . . . a Knight-errant of human folly and the dream of ambition . . . caught up in my own selfhood . . . and its involving masquerade of the changeling nicknamed Free Will.

But I will have the wisdom of the fool, at least, who wisely owns his vanity and his foolishness . . . and what more can any man aspire to?

In life you have to feel your way . . . you touch it only with the heart.

Oh, god . . . Sandy's falling . . . I must brace myself to take the pull on the rope . . . stand in . . . lean back . . . only a '*free stance*' . . .

The last man absolutely must not fall . . .

Ah! My ankle . . . god, my leg's gone from under me . . . I'm falling . . . falling

XXXIV

Hell's teeth . . . what a bloody awful mess . . . I've grabbed and clawed myself to a stop, a bloody, painfully gradual arrest of fall by hand check and body friction . . . the exacting, brutal mercies of rock to gravity.

Poor bloody Sandy . . . the ideal companion . . . a chap to depend on . . . our experiment to get one superman. Superb physique . . . colossal red corpuscles . . . everything except conversation. The winning spirit . . . the star of the new members. As stout a heart as you could find. Oh, hell and buggeration! What can quiet us in a death . . .

What can . . . god in damnation . . .

No merciful straw of consolation . . .

Only the heaven rending loss . . .

And all that we had achieved . . .

It's all gone to hell . . . bloody crud . . .

The great venture . . . our terrific go . . . down the ruddy *khud* . . .

XXXV

Damn it, I'm not comfortable lying here . . . Sod it, the pain in my right arm . . . and buggering hell, the old ankle's absolutely bloody crocked again . . . I'll just put my good leg over lightly and try, somehow to ease it, if possible, into a less painful position.

To be as comfortable as you can is a basic principle of climbing . . .

Only I don't feel quite myself . . . everything seems a long way off . . . I'm sitting on the merry-go-round . . . waiting for Sandy to come and jump into his seat . . . It's funny but I keep thinking I'm going to wake up.

Now I'm making sand pies in the garden . . . what fun, a perfect sand pie . . . so beautiful . . . my earliest memory . . . that plumply satisfying symmetry . . . suddenly a small section breaks off and falls from the top . . . It's such an awful sight to see . . . I don't know why it's so disturbing.

The left side of my head aches so . . .

I really must try and get moving . . .

I can't just lie here forever . . .

To lose my pains . . .

My last hope . . .

XXXVI

For just frightful seconds I fell . . . down the damn mountainside . . . out of the glory and the dream . . . all the history of such a day . . . down to this dark edge of life.

Where the sea of Time and Space runs down . . .

Full fathom five . . . the final deposition . . .

This was a seabed on which my body settles,
now the tide of events leaves me for wrack . . .

as time turns from me on the ebb of memory.

Flotsam of the backwash, no longer current,
soon I too will only be a still rumour of the sea . . .

my empty shell softly sounding the silent reach
of surcease and oblivion . . . softly as any snow.

I couldn't see myself coming down defeated . . .

Only angels ever died at this height before . . .

No need for the forgotten compass . . .

zeroed out now as I am . . .

Death boxes the rose at all points.

Nothing heals at altitude . . .

no quarter for the injured here.

Naught broken save this body . . .

save this body which cannot . . .

but among the great sleeping ones . . .

XXXVII

Now dully through my numb ears rumours the keening wind, its frostbiting edge feels blunt. Pain's urgency is only for the living.

The fitful, feeble rhythm of my heart, once pregnant with celestial fire, guttering into discordant fibrillation. The creeping crepitation of the ice . . .

Where is the Comforter now?

My sluggish blood will begin to crystallise, turning my flesh into a gelid tomb of ice.

When my heart is frozen, crystal cold as stone . . . let it be to the mountain, so tempered and indurate, we'll meet as obdurate equals . . . with all the grave time of stones.

In winter, I'll have a sepulchre of snow. How that image graves upon the mind.

Tutankhamun had a wreath of cornflowers, but I'll lie open to the zodiac of the stars.

Slowly, I shall return to the elements . . . the last informity of the mineral king-dom.

My fingers almost rooted in the rocks, clung so once tenaciously for life. All those years they'd felt and sought for holds, against the stubborn, smooth and slippery rock. In climbing I had a very graceful style. Youth is unaware of the slipperiness of reputation.

Those heady, Alpine days of promising form, mountains in an almost civilised country. Not like the rude and peasant squalor of Tibet. Nothing could have prepared me for the Himalayas.

Undulating on this last inflorescence of memory . . . the mind's eye view of it all in such perspective.

High up in these desiccating temperatures, my body will remain preserved as a mummy, embalmed by the arefaction of the freezing cold. Snowfalls will come and go upon me . . .

I will be as concerned as any star.

Wind and weather will whittle and abrade, fretting and fraying my redundant clothing, until, denuded by gales and cyclonic storms, my ancient, frozen flesh will be scoured, burnished to a snow-blinding whiteness.

So posterity will find and intrude upon me.

I will still look impossibly young for my age. My marmoreal body marred but still classical, lying forlornly in the shadow of Everest's awesome, north face of starkly snow denuded rock. As hallowed almost then, by the years, as a saintly relic . . .

The reliquary testimony of body language eloquent, at the last, of my final moments.

Others will come, I shall not be alone forever, this I know is more certain than any simple faith. As long as the challenge remains, men will come.

Human courage in its stubborn perseverance, magnificent and absurd . . . the undying paradoxical rhyme of life.

Let me hymn adversity as only the wind . . .

XXXVIII

The ebbing current now of the soul . . . a fading pulse in the eternal mind.

My last, faint, scandent thoughts . . .

That first view of Everest from the top of the Pang La . . . beyond the reach of words . . . the inexpressible way it caught the spirit . . . up into such a longing and desire . . . and I was wearing two felt hats to keep out the cold.

Memory comes and ghosts . . . these precious haunts of life . . .

All the ways of my heart in the mountains . . .

The old Miners' Track and the causeway . . . the fabled, snowy mountain of King Arthur, the Hill of Awen . . . the Hill of the Muse . . . and the white flowers of grass of Parnassus . . .

And my climbing roots in the enduring rock.

Geoffrey said I would be ticketed after Everest . . . the fame of it a magic open sesame . . .

To speak the name of the dead is to make them live again . . .

Yes. . . such an awfully big adventure . . . I didn't lose sight of the 'rightness of the attempt' . . . only too far into the unknown at the limits of endurance . . .

Ah, God to see the branches stir . . .

Across a summer sky, cattle chumbling clover in a meadow, with skylarks hanging on by song, somewhere heavenward above, as if they sought the ear of God. I always hungered for the heights . . . a deep homesickness of the soul.

Those fledgling days in the high Alps . . . getting mountain sickness on my first day on Mont Vélan and throwing up . . . but I had found the way into the heart of myself . . . the quick of my being . . . and the snow was like swansdown, gemmed with sparkling spangles. A world of coruscating light . . . an aura of angels . . . the air of revelation . . . the *altum silentium* of a pristine world.

To smell the thrilling-sweet and rotten
Unforgettable, unforgotten
River smell . . .

Rowing . . . rowing home to haven, the sound of oars creaking in rowlocks, then dipping swift, quicksilver in the slurp and slappy water. Now swinging out and round dripping, feathered into sunlight and Quiet kind.

Ruth's face so patient now and loving . . .

O, dear girl, my dearest love . . . I am beyond time . . . and even your forgiveness.

Now fades the glimmering mindscape . . .

I leave the world in darkness and to be . . .

The bells have begun . . . armistice . . .

Armistice wrung out at last . . .

in all its solemn riot of poppies . . .

The never to be forgotten . . .

Old friends seen again . . .

The immortal river still . . .

It was more like war than mountaineering . . .

Never mind Everest . . .

I came through London in carpet slippers and no hat . . .

Father will never forget it.

For the Background:
Notes to part I

Geoffrey Winthrop Young (1876 – 1958) Mallory's climbing mentor. They met for the first time in 1909, at the Charles Lamb Dinner in Cambridge. Young said that they 'became fast friends at once' and he invited him to Wales to climb with him. And Mallory duly became one of the star members of Young's 'Hill Company', attending the regular meets at Pen-y-Pass. In 1920 Young wrote *Mountain Craft*, which was reviewed by Mallory in the *Climbers' Club Journal.* In the review Mallory said that it was 'the most important work on mountaineering which has appeared in this generation'. And Walt Unsworth,* in the *Encyclopaedia of Mountaineering*, says that 'it was for long the standard work'. At the start of the entry in the *Encyclopaedia*, Young is described simply as 'one of the most important figures in British mountaineering'. His was one of the shaping influences in Mallory's life. And it was Young who first mentioned the idea of Everest to him and subsequently, it was he who managed to talk Mallory's wife, Ruth round to accepting the idea of his going on the Everest Reconnaissance Expedition in 1921. Young thought that 'a fine climb is an artistic creation' and said that 'mountaineering must be judged by a spiritual, not a utilitarian, standard'. He also wanted climbers to guard against 'the fatal crowd infection of judging results above the spirit and manner of the doing'.

In his early days at Cambridge, he was the anonymous author of *The Roof–Climber's Guide to Trinity,* a guide for students wishing to tackle the challenge of the spires of the college, under the cover of darkness. With the guide Josef Knubel he did a number of outstanding climbs, for their day, in the Alps. He led an 'amateur rope' (i.e. without a professional guide) on the first ascent of the Nesthorn with Donald Robertson & George Mallory in 1909, that is referred to in the narrative. While serving with an ambulance unit in the First World War he lost his left leg. Although he invented an artificial limb and gamely continued to climb after the war, he was obviously not able to go on the Everest expeditions in the 1920s as a result. *Mountaincraft* was one of the books I drew on to get a feel for the climbing background at the time, the 'cutting edge' of it then, and have quoted from it, as Mallory would have known it so well. And, also of course, *The Roof-Climber's Guide to Trinity.*

* c.f. See Walt Unsworth's *Encyclopaedia of Mountaineering*, Hodder & Stoughton 1992

Notes to part II

Both of the quotations are from Shelley, the first Mallory himself quoted in his article *Our 1919 Journey* in the *Alpine Journal*, 33, pp.166–185, Nov. 1920. The second, beginning 'Thou hast a voice great Mountain, to repeal' is taken from *Mont Blanc*. Mallory greatly admired Mont Blanc itself and nursed an ambition to make a first ascent by the Peuterey Ridge. And Shelley was his favourite poet. The first ascent of Mont Blanc by the Peuterey Ridge was done in 1927: three years after Mallory's death, by L. Obersteiner & K. Schreiner.

Notes to part IV

English air – was the 'homely' term that the Sherpas gave to the oxygen that was breathed from the high-pressure, gas cylinders.

The fact that Mallory cannot remember the words to Gray's *Elegy Written in a Country Churchyard,* is used as a device here to indicate that he is experiencing the effects of altitude. Subsequently, on the following day of the climb, as a result of his effort to remember, lines from Gray's *Elegy* will come back into his mind. To many readers the *Elegy,* with its slow-moving stanzas and its quiet, twilight meditation on life – the paths of glory – and death, will be a much-loved poem, as it was for Mallory. And as those who know the poem will know, it is in the tradition of graveyard contemplation and was composed initially in the churchyard at St Andrew's, Stoke Poges. The following entry for the 9th of May 1924, in Mallory's journal-style letter to his wife Ruth, is both touching and illuminating. It is evening and Mallory and three other members of the expedition are huddled in a tent:

'I produced *The Spirit of Man* and began reading one thing and another. Howard reminded me that I was reproducing on the same spot a scene which occurred two years ago when he and I lay together. We all agreed that *Kubla Khan* was a good sort of poem. Irvine was rather poetry-shy, but seemed to be favourably impressed by the Epitaph to Gray's *Elegy*. Odell was much inclined to be interested and liked the last lines of *Prometheus Unbound*. S., who knows a lot of English literature, had never read a poem of Emily Brontë's and was happily introduced. – And suddenly soup arrived.'

Quotations from the above mentioned poems and others from the anthology compiled by Robert Bridges *The Spirit of Man* (1915), which Mallory had first with him on the Western Front, and then subsequently took on all of the three Everest Expeditions, occur throughout the book, as Mallory obviously would have known most of the poems in it so well.

Notes to Part V

George Finch (1888–1970) – Failed the medical examination for the 1921 Everest Reconnaissance expedition – 'very deficient in teeth'. An early advocate of the need to use oxygen; he was selected for and designated to be the Oxygen Officer on the 1922 Everest Expedition. For which he designed his own jacket out of parachute silk and eiderdown and in his patent climbing outfit, demonstrated the use of the gas apparatus while being photographed by the official photographer. This was considered to be a huge joke by all of the climbing community at the time: *the shape of things to come* ... and everyone just laughed in derision. Mallory was later to take to heart what he saw Finch achieve on the 1922 Expedition. And subsequently studied Finch's account, which included a description of rigging up the gas apparatus so that it could be used practicably in a tent. On their summit attempt, using oxygen, Finch with Geoffrey Bruce, reached the highest point on the mountain 27,300ft– the highest man had climbed at that time. The fact that Finch was not selected for the 1924 Expedition was a shabby and shameful affair; an account of it all is provided by Walt Unsworth in his book *Everest,* regarded as the definitive history. It is known that Mallory was planning to visit Finch, on his return from Everest, to honourably acknowledge his debt to him.

Memento mori – Remember that you must die (Latin – literally remember to die) anything (e.g. skull) to remind one of mortality.

Notes to part VI

Yet once more, O ye Mountain, and once more
Ye Snow frigid with Icy, frosty hoar,
I reach toward your virgin Summit core,
Let not thy rude, inclement winds be too frore.

Readers of my generation and older will recognise this as a parody of the beginning of Milton's elegy *Lycidas,* which begins:

Yet once more, O ye Laurels, and once more
Ye Myrtles brown with Ivy never-sear,
I com to pluck your Berries harsh and crude,
And with forc'd fingers rude ...

And in common with generations of schoolteachers in England, Mallory taught Milton's poetry. For those of a younger generation and who have not read English Literature at University: John Milton (1608 – 1674) – A puritan and supporter of the Parliamentary Cause against King Charles 1. Later a Republican and official poet during the period of the Commonwealth under Oliver Cromwell. His elegy *Lycidas,* a highly formal yet individual elegy, that fuses Classical, Christian and personal elements, was for the premature death of a talented young friend. Even those who do not know Milton at all, will probably recognise the phrase 'fame is the spur', which comes from it. In the following observation on part of the underlying psychology behind climbing, Mallory himself quoted just those lines from *Lycidas* from which the familiar quote comes.

The desire to climb mountains is commonly held among laymen to be an incomprehensible psychological freak. One explanation, nevertheless, is commonly given – that we climb to win admiration. No mountaineer will accept that. And yet, when he remembers that the admiration is freely offered, he may forget that the admiration is not completely withheld. Or, in mere indignation at its inadequacy, he may neglect it altogether. It is incomplete, of course, but it is probably true to say of most mountaineers, as one among several reasons, that they climb to win admiration:

Fame is the spur that the clear spirit doth raise
To scorn delights and live laborious days ...

'Fame' we call it for those with whose motives we are apt to sympathise; and for the others – 'Advertisement' or 'Low Competitive Spirit'.

George Mallory

An unpublished fragment quoted in D. Robertson's biography, *George Mallory.*

In the course of the poem Milton struggles to make sense of life in the face of death. Concluding that one meets the grief of personal loss by the assertion of purpose. Milton wrote a major epic poem *Paradise Lost,* 'to justify the ways of God to Man'. Which had a profound influence on William Blake who acknowledged him as a spiritual teacher. (See notes for Part XV). Once accorded classic status and revered, Milton's work is now rather out of fashion.

The legendary Mummery: Albert Frederick Mummery (1855–1895). Considered by Martin Conway to be 'the greatest climber of his, or any other generation', but Winthrop Young thought that his achievements were overrated. On the subject of making such judgements, he had written, in a more considered and reflective mood in *Mountain Craft*. 'A chronicler must always face the dilemma whether or not the great man by his example produces the general change of practice, or whether to class him as the conspicuous anticipatory ripple of the general current of coming change'. Walt Unsworth says of Mummery, that he has 'justifiable claims to being the founder of modern Alpinism'. To begin with Mummery climbed with a guide, Alexander Burgener, and converted to guideless climbing around 1860 ('the Englishman likes to find his own way to heaven'). His famous 'easy day for a lady' was a traverse of the Grépon, which he made with Cecil Slingsby & Miss Bristow in 1893. The quote comes from the heading of Ch. 6 of his book: *The Grépon. An inaccessible peak – The most difficult climb in the Alps – An easy day for a lady*. The three stages, he thought, that all mountains were doomed to go through. This is what Mallory, in the text, refers to as 'Mummery's Law'. The book *My Climbs in the Alps and Caucusus* (1895) became a classic of climbing literature. And Unsworth says of the last chapter 'The Pleasures and Penalties of Mountaineering', which contains Mummery's climbing philosophy, 'that it showed the way the sport had to develop'. He goes on to say that 'it had a profound influence, *most notably on the continent'* (my italics). Interestingly, on his famous first ascent of the Teufelsgrat, on the Täschhorn, he was accompanied by his wife, and it is Mrs Mummery's account of the climb that appears in his book. Notwithstanding his 'easy day for a lady' quip, Fred Mummery seems to have been an early pioneer of equal opportunities as well as climbing.

He had made an attempt on the Diamiri face, before he disappeared on Nanga Parbat, together with his two Gurkha companions Raghobir and Goman Singh, on the 24th of August 1895.

Notes to part VII

Whizz-bang – An onomatopoeic term for a light shell fired from one of the smaller field-artillery guns – the British 18-pounder, the French 75 millimetre and the German 77 millimetre were all in this category. Due to the low trajectory of these guns, whizz-bangs arrived as soon, if not sooner, than they were heard.

Fathom Five – torrential rains had flooded the drainage system around the O.P. dug–out and as a result of the water now in the bottom of it, Mallory called it 'Fathom Five'. . . from the song, of course, in Shakespeare's play *The Tempest.*

O. P. i.e. Observation Post & the term 'O. Pipping' was derived from the Signalese for O.P. It was often difficult to pass messages accurately over a field telephone and in order to differentiate similar sounds a system, known as Signalese, was devised by which A became *Ack,* and B – *Beer*, D – *Don*, M – *Emma*, P – *pip* etc. Hence the Pip in O. P. And thus Signalese for p.m. would be – Pip Emma.

On hearing of Rupert Brooke's death, Mallory wrote to A. C. Benson:

'Rupert Brooke is dead of blood poisoning. I expect my friends to be killed in battle, but not that way. It seems so wanton, and somehow a blow under the belt. He was a loveable person, and besides he had great gifts. I never much thought that he had it in him to be a great poet, but after all he might have become one.'

Siegfried Herford (1896–1916): On December 27th, 1914, together with Mallory & Winthrop Young he did the Double Girdle Traverse of Lliwedd. The single traverse, across the north face from Far East Buttress to the Slanting Buttress, had been described by Andrews & Thomson in the guidebook, as 'presenting problems so numerous and varied in character that they feed the appetite for novelty with perpetual gratifications'. And such was their enjoyment, that they dropped down a ridge and then re-crossed the whole face once more, 'over bastion, wall and chasm'.

Of his climb of the Central Buttress on Scafell, including the famous Flake Crack in 1914, Alan Hankinson writes in *Camera on the Crags*: 'The current guide book says it was 'probably the biggest single breakthrough in standard in the history of Lakeland climbing'. The route affords 475 feet of climbing of unrelenting difficulty; it is graded 'Very Severe (Hard)': it is the most popular climb on Scafell.'

It is now known that Siegfried Herford was killed by a rifle-grenade at Festubert. His family believed that he had been killed by a sniper's bullet. Which, if you think about it, is exactly what any decent C.O. would have told them in his letter of condolence at the time, thus sparing family and friends the grisly and unnecessary detail. From a letter to his wife, cited by the Gillmans in their biography of Mallory on p.132, it seems that Mallory thought that Herford had been killed at Ypres. At the beginning of 1916, the two major British battles of the First World War had been First Ypres 1914 &

Second Ypres 1915 (the Battle of the Somme started on July 1st 1916 and Passchendaele – Third Ypres would begin in July 1917).

Ypres, the old capital of Flanders, and the defensive salient set up around the city assumed a symbolic significance in the war beyond any military value. In the words of Field-Marshal the Earl of Ypres, Sir Charles Harington and Field-Marshal the Lord Plumer of Messines in the foreword to *The Battle Book of Ypres*: 'Ypres does not stand for a ruined town, but for a very high ideal built up of the lives of men'.

The Germans used chlorine gas ('clouds of yellow-green smoke') for the first time at the Second Battle of Ypres and deployed the heaviest concentration of their big artillery, guns that fired a 42-centimetre shell (a calibre roughly equivalent to our 16-inch) that became known as a 'wipers express'. Robin Neillands, in his recent book *The Great War Generals on the Western Front 1914-1918,* assessing the total cost of the Second Battle of Ypres to the British, Canadian & Indian forces involved provides the following chilling figure – 59, 275 men killed, wounded or missing. He concludes the chapter in his book on Second Ypres with the question: 'who in Europe, nine months before Second Ypres, could have imagined such a battle and such slaughter?'

It is understandable therefore that Mallory, writing to his wife in February 1916, still within the ominous shadow of the aftermath of Second Ypres, might well have assumed that Herford had fallen there. Indeed it seems to have been a widespread and general belief amongst the climbing fraternity, as Walt Unsworth, in the *Encyclopaedia of Mountaineering* (1992), states firmly that he was killed at Ypres. A pessimistic remark though of Edmund Blunden's, in his memoir *Undertones of War,* capturing the mood of 1917, I think sheds some light on this, by revealing the extent and degree of the ill-fated sense of foreboding about the place: 'We shall all die, presumably, around Ypres'. This was written at the time of Passchendaele.

At the end of the war, the Ypres League was formed: ' To perpetuate the tradition of the four years defence of the Salient as an ideal, and a source of inspiration for all time'. And the first historical guide to Ypres, published in the early 1920s under its auspices, was entitled: *The Immortal Salient.*

Clausewitz, Carl Philipp Gottlieb von – His masterpiece *On War,* first published in 1832, remains the most famous, classic study of the nature and conditions of warfare. Clausewitz endeavours to present an historical understanding of war, 'to show how every age had its own kind of war, its own limiting conditions, and its own preconceptions'. And that 'the events of every age must therefore be judged in the light of its own peculiarities'. While presenting a philosophical analysis of the actual conduct and experience of war. It is a fascinating work, full of illuminating and memorable insights (*'Tension & Rest – The dynamic law of war'. 'All thinking is art, etc'.*). I have chosen the following as a sample illustration; wherein readers who are also are climbers may see certain parallels:

'If we take a general view of the four elements composing the atmosphere in which war moves, of *danger*, *physical effort, uncertainty*, and *chance*, it is easy to conceive that a great force of mind and understanding is requisite to be able to make way with safety and success amongst such opposing elements, a force which, according to the different modifications arising out of circumstances, we find termed by military writers and annalists as *energy, firmness, strength of mind and character.*'

Editions of abridged versions of Clausewitz's *On War* are available in both Penguin Classics & Wordsworth Classics. Beatrice Heuser, Professor of Strategic and International Studies in the Department of War Studies at King's College, London, has recently written an interesting study of the man and the book, *Reading Clausewitz* (Pimlico, London, 2002).

The harrowing of those hours of sacrifice . . . Mallory was, as he narrates in the text, with a siege Artillery Battery at Albert on the day the Fourth Army advanced. They were all volunteers, most of them members of locally recruited 'Pal's Battalions', who had responded to the nation's call to arms. As many readers will know, the casualty figures for the first day of the Battle of the Somme made a total of 57, 470 men, of whom 19,240 were killed. In *The Imperial War Museum Book of the Somme*, Malcolm Brown, in the conclusion to his account of the 1st of July 1916, says of the appalling toll, that 'it is destined to be a subject of continuing controversy'. The Welsh artist and poet, David Jones, who served in the Welsh Fusiliers during the battle, said that the Nineteenth Century died in the mud on the Somme. The bitter winter weather finally brought the battle, or to be more exact, the bloody succession of battles to a close on the 19th of November. In the words of *The Official History*:

'Here, in a wilderness of mud, holding water-logged trenches or shell-hole posts, accessible only by night, the infantry abode in conditions which might be likened to those of earthworms rather than human kind. Our vocabulary is not adapted to describe such an existence, because it is outside experience for which words are normally required. Mud, for the men in the line, was no mere inorganic nuisance and obstacle. It took on an aggressive, wolf-like guise, and like a wolf could pull down the lonely wanderer in the darkness.'

'Our vocabulary is not adapted to describe' says it all. The standard estimate of casualties of all types for the Battle of the Somme is 498,054. But John Mosier has recently pointed out in his book *The Myth of the Great War,* that this figure apparently omits the 'diversionary' offensives to the north, most notably the Aubreville Ridge, thus it is very likely that it is too low.

On the 20th of July 1916 Mallory wrote to his wife: 'The journalistic capital which the halfpenny press is making out of the war just now – well, 'I have a sort of disgust for it, like for vomit and such'.

Roll on, Duration – The duration of the war. The volunteers of 1914–15, with whom Mallory was among, enlisted for three years or the duration of the war – which, as John Brophy & Eric Partridge point out in their book, *The Long Trail – What the British soldier sang and said 1914-1918,* is an ambiguous phrase. And they go on to explain that this was a source of endless argument among optimists who expected the end to come, each successive year, *by the following Christmas* (my italics). The heartfelt expression – 'Roll on, Duration' they gloss with the following *translation* into plain English: 'God end the war and make me a civilian again'. A prayer that must have been on many a soldiers' lips.

Boswell & the anecdote – comes as Mallory says in the text, from his biographical study *Boswell the Biographer,* which was published by Smith, Elder & Co in 1912.

In the book Mallory wrote of Boswell: 'it is the candour of Boswell far more than any other single factor, the natural instinct to record what he observed both of himself and of others, the honesty in observing and truthfulness which he had as an artist in recording, that distinguishes his literary work. Herein lay the essence of his genius'.

A Pfaltz of tender blue ... and the ruddy song in question: the song is about a P.B.O. (P.B.O. = *Poor bloody observer*) and entitled: *YOU'RE ONLY A P.B.O.* Sung to the tune of "*A Bachelor Gay*" from "*The Maid of the Mountains*" (a big musical show hit, certainly before most readers' time). And the first two lines of the chorus go:

At seventeen he's shooting rather badly at a *Pfaltz* of tender blue,

At fifteen thou. you see him point out sadly some Huns of a different hue,

From the *Airman's Song Book*, p. 47, ed. by C.H. Ward & Leighton Lucas. London, 1967.

And the *Pfaltz?* – The *Pfaltz* 'of tender blue' was a German, single seater fighter aircraft; a biplane that was armed with two machine guns.

Zeppelin – As many readers will know, was a German airship ('a monster gas-bag inflated with inflammable hydrogen gas') named after Graf Ferdinand Von Zeppelin; a visionary of the lighter-than-air school of aeronautics. The *Graf* made the first flight with a rigid airship, *L.Z.I (Luftschiff Zeppelin),* on 2nd of July 1900, over Lake Constance. Eight years later, at the end of 1908, the Zeppelin Airship Company Ltd. was formed in Friedrichshafen. The Kaiser personally decorated the *Graf* with the Order of the Black Eagle, calling him the 'greatest German of the century'. The German Army & Navy were issued with the latest *Zeppelin* airships in 1913. They looked menacingly like being 'the new terror weapons' of the age.

At the beginning of the war in Britain, 'Zepp raids' were fearfully anticipated. And after a whole month had passed without even a sighting, a sinister rumour began that a *Zeppelin* was hidden in the Lake District – just outside Grasmere! And it was widely believed that this skulking dirigible took off every night, from its remote and scenic fastness, to carry out reconnaissance flights over Bristol, London, and the Portsmouth dockyards. Only after Lieutenant B. C. Hucks, flying a Bleriot-11, had carried out a thorough aerial reconnaissance of the whole area, were these reports discounted. The 'infernal machine' was not profaning the hallowed haunt of our Romantic poets, nor casting its sinister shadow over the beloved crags. But the rumour vividly illustrates the extent to which the *Zeppelin* was a 'bogey weapon' in the minds of the British people in 1914.

The first *Zeppelin* raid took place on January 19th, 1915, and both Yarmouth and King's Lynn were bombed. The strongest reaction from the rest of world, to the first deliberate raid on undefended cities came from the United States. The editorial in the *New York Herald* ran: "Is this the madness of despair or just plain everyday madness that has prompted the Germans to select for attack peaceful and undefended resorts on the English coast?" In fairness it must be remembered that the Germans were trying to hit strategic targets, but that memorable phrase, *the madness of despair,* has an awful resonance for our own time.

London was bombed from the air by the German Army *L.Z. 38*, commanded by

Hauptmann Linnarz on the night of May 31st 1915. And further concerted *Zeppelin* bombing raids followed. An American reporter, William G. Shepherd's description of the raid on the night of September 8th, 1915, vividly captures the reality of it at the time:

'Suddenly you realise that the biggest city in the world has become a night battlefield in which 7,000,000 harmless men, women and children live. Here is war at the very heart of civilisation, threatening all the millions of things that human hearts and minds have created in past centuries.'

During the first six months of 1916, forty-six *Zeppelins* crossed the British coastline between Yorkshire and Kent on bombing raids. And London was attacked again on two, separate occasions. But by the summer of 1916 the Home Defence squadrons were issued with new incendiary ammunition. A combination of an incendiary bullet, a phosphorous bullet and an explosive bullet, of which one German airship commander said, "This pattern of incendiary ammunition was an invention of the devil". And thus the tide of the *Zeppelin* menace was turned back.

Zeppelin crews were amongst the first to experience the problems of altitude and to breathe oxygen from cylinders. One of the later generation of height climbers, *L58* equipped with the Maybach MBIVa 'altitude motors', climbed to 19,700 feet in 1917. (The current altitude record in the climbing world at the time was held by the Duke of Abruzzi; who had made the ascent of Bride Peak, 24,697 feet, in the Karakoram in 1909). The *Zeppelin* crews apparently thought that the only food that was agreeable at low temperatures was chocolate.

Robinson, Douglas H. *The Zeppelin in Combat.* U.S.A., 1994. Poolman, Kenneth. *Zeppelins Over England.* London, 1960. Whitehouse, Arch. *The Zeppelin Fighters.* London, 1968. Botting, Douglas. *Dr. Eckener's Dream Machine.* New York, 2001.

Fred Karno's Air Corps was the title of a parodic song sung in every *R.F.C.* (Royal Flying Corps) mess. It was sung to the tune of *'The Church's One Foundation'*. And the following excerpt will have to suffice to provide a sense of the droll spirit of it.

We are Fred Karno's air corps,
We are the R.F.C.
We cannot fly,
We cannot shoot,
What ruddy use are we?

The song, of course, ends on a more positively affirmative note.
Airman's Song Book, p.17.

Fred Karno was a theatrical impresario, comedian and leader of the most outstanding company of comics and comedy actors before the First World War. He built a theatrical enterprise of more than thirty companies, whose repertoire included Christmas pantomimes and elaborate comedies. He had a huge reputation in America and his shows attracted headline attention. His name was a by word for any comic outfit at the time, as Monty Python is in ours. The most famous protégé out of his troupe was Charlie Chaplin, who went to America with him in one his shows.

Notes to section VIII

Mt. Woolworth – At the time of Mallory's lecture tour, the Woolworth Building on 233 Broadway, Lower Manhattan, was the highest building in New York. It was 58 storeys high but the storeys were so large, it was in sheer scale, more in the region of 79–80 storeys. And the man behind it was, of course, the five & dime store man himself, Mr. Frank Woolworth, to the tune of $13 million. Work started in 1910 and it was opened in 1913. It was not superseded in height until 1931. It is still called the Woolworth Building.

Safety Last – Harold Lloyd's greatest comedy stunt climbing up a skyscraper, still rightly regarded as a comic masterpiece. Shows what a comic genius can do with a minimal budget, but ideally only for those with a good head for heights. Harold Lloyd did all his own stunts and *they were for real* – mostly.

The Ten Commandments – made into a hugely successful Hollywood epic in 1923, directed by Cecil B. DeMille – hence Mallory's joke about it being 'old hat' now. For Mallory in 1924, it was last year's sensation.

Donald Robertson (1880?–1910) was a friend & climbing companion of Mallory's. In 1909 he climbed the Nesthorn and the Jungfrau, together with Mallory & Winthrop Young. And they then made an attempt on the precipitous walls of the aiguilles above the Mer de Glâce. He wrote an article for the *Alpine Journal* entitled *Alpine Humour*, from whence I have taken the quotation. It was in this article that Mallory perhaps got the seed-crystal for his comparison of a day in the Alps to a symphony.

'For the matters of common knowledge in mountaineering are the emotions which form its very blood. The night in the gite or hut, the rise in the dark, the tramp in the wake of the lantern, sunrise, the concert-piece of the day – scherzo, allegro, andante cantabile, andante maestoso, terminating in the coda of after years.'

I have taken and quoted his phrase 'the masquerade of the changeling nicknamed Free Will' on two separate occasions. I thought that it was too striking and memorable to leave it, in his own words, 'in the place of bones'. And I have also used, towards the end, his rather poignant and touching description of the mountains as 'the great sleeping ones'; 'he is not the greatest but the least of things, among the great sleeping ones who have but to stir in their slumber and he sleeps with them'. Which, of course, Mallory himself quoted.

The article was published at the beginning of March 1910 in the *A.J.* and at Easter of that same year Donald Robertson fell, while leading up the Eastern Gully of Glyder Fach. Tragically there was no coda of after years. He died as a result of a fractured skull. Educated at Eton & Trinity (Cantab.), he was Secretary of the Royal Commission on Electoral Systems. Winthrop Young felt that his death 'darkened the hills with clouds that never again quite dispersed'. Pointing out the often fatal consequences of a slip in those days, Peter & Leni Gillman, in their biography of Mallory, state that 'today's climbers, who would have placed a running belay and worn a helmet, would almost certainly have survived'. At the end of *Alpine Humour* Donald Robertson himself had written:

'The faith of a mountaineer is, and must be, that a life lost in the legitimate pursuit of our aims is not a life thrown away, but a forfeit of a stake set for an exceeding great reward, the rendering up of a soul to the hills that made it a worthy sacrifice.'

Tutankhamun – Almost immediately after the discovery in November 1922 of the boy king's un-robbed tomb – 'Wonderful things – I can see wonderful things' in the famous words of Howard Carter – 'Egyptianism' became all the rage. An inspirational source for the kitsch of Art Deco and by 1923 the craze for the 'ancient Egyptian-style' extended from fashionable ladies hats to Huntley & Palmer biscuit tins. And at the British Empire Exhibition in 1924, you could not only see a scale model of Mt. Everest, you could also go and visit a large scale replica of the original, young pharaoh's tomb, bearing the sign outside, 'TOMB OF TUT– ANKH – AMEN' – and all within Wembley Park. The two models were among the main competing attractions.

The scale model of Mt. Everest at the British Empire Exhibition, is an indication of the degree to which the mountain had captured the popular imagination and is eloquent of the optimistic expectation that the 'Third Pole' would be conquered that year.

Walter Pater (1839-94) Still a deeply out-of-fashion, Victorian writer, aesthetician and art critic. Perhaps possibly best known now because Oscar Wilde was perceived as being one of his disciples. He wrote in a finely crafted, 'musically languorous prose style'. His *Studies in the History of the Renaissance,* first published in 1873, is still around in paper-back editions. W. B. Yeats included the well-known passage from it on the Mona Lisa, in his edition of the Oxford Book of Modern Verse. When Mallory was just up at Cam-bridge in 1905, Pater's work would still be being read and discussed. And Mallory's tutor at Cambridge, A.C.Benson had written a study of Pater, which Mallory, therefore, was obliged to read. The conclusion to Pater's *Renaissance* probably remains the best known and oft quoted, as it was seen as being 'a philosophy of sensationalist hedonism' and thus providing a licence for the decadence of the 1890s. The man himself was a rather timid Oxford recluse.

Robot – 1923 saw the first production on the London stage of a new play by a Czecho-slovakian writer & playwright, Carel Capek. The play was *R.U.R.* (Rossum's Universal Robots). And a new word – robot, which Capek had invented from the Czech *robota* – statute labour, entered the language . . . and the imagination. The film *I, Robot* is essentially the same story, but it lacks the freshness, originality and the intelligence of the original.

Notes to Section XI

Martin Conway (1856 – 1937) 'A scholar should know all about some subjects and something about all subjects'. So wrote the scholar Martin Conway, who was an art historian and critic, writer and explorer: who believed in the efficacy and benefits of Bovril, Brandy, Vaseline and Eucalyptus Jujubes. Understandably for his time and artis-tic temperament, he had a romantic attitude and approach to the hills. For him moun-tains were more than just 'a casual assemblage of crags affording gymnastic problems'. The Alps 'has led me into regions of such fairy beauty that the fabled wonders of Xanadu seem commonplace beside them'. In 1895 he wrote *The Alps from End to End,* which was widely admired and influential in its time. 'New comers to the hills always underestimate, magnitude and distances. *The beginner has to learn size by disappointment* (my italics)'. He considered the *Zermatt Pocket Book* to be 'the pemmican of Alpine literature'. And later he deplored how badly dressed people were in the Alpine resorts. Definitely not adding to the beauty of scenes. In 1892 he organised the first major climbing expedition to go to the Himalaya, and selected the Karakoram district. One of the young members on that expedition, was a young Gurkha officer, Lt. C. G. Bruce, who would later lead both the 1922 & 1924 Everest Expeditions. (The Everest Expeditions were modelled upon Conway's expedition). Towards the end of his life, Conway sadly bemoaned, that 'the mystery is gone from the Alps'.

To struggle and to understand – Some readers may recognise this quotation as it comes from the once very well known ending to an article Mallory wrote for the *Alpine Journal – Mont Blanc from the Col du Géant.* He wrote it at the Western Front, 'writing the account of an expedition in the Alps from an unaided memory'. Such was the measure of the time – and his article was published in the *A.J.*(32) in September 1918. The article concludes with the party reaching the summit of Mont Blanc:

'Is this the summit, crowning the day? How cool and quiet! We're not exultant; but delighted, joyful; soberly astonished . . . Have we vanquished an enemy? None but ourselves. Have we gained success? That word means nothing here. Have we won a kingdom? No . . . and yes. We have achieved an ultimate satisfaction . . . fulfilled a destiny . . . To struggle and to understand – never this last without the other; such is the law . . .'

I have read that climbers of an older generation used to quote this to one another – especially whilst sharing the joy of a summit.

The secret strength of things ... a quotation once again from Shelley's poem *Mont Blanc.*

Einstein at the time – in November 1919, as a result of the confirmation that light waves are bent by the gravitational field of the earth, provided by Arthur Eddington's photographs of the total eclipse of the sun, taken in Principe, the *Times* carried the headline 'REVOLUTION IN SCIENCE. NEW THEORY OF THE UNIVERSE'. And day after day the world's press ran editorials and features about Einstein. He was universally acclaimed as a hero and a genius. In his book *Einstein and the Total Eclipse,* Peter Coles, Prof. of Astrophysics at the University of Nottingham, suggests that a factor in Einstein's extraordinary popular rise to mythic status at the time, was the stark nature of the other news events that otherwise were dominating world attention. And cites the following headlines: ARMISTICE AND TREATY TERMS; GERMANS SUMMONED TO PARIS; and WAR CRIMES AGAINST SERBIA.

Notes to Part XII

Younghusband, Sir Francis (1863 – 1942) Chairman of the Everest Committee – An extraordinary character, 'Man of Action, Man of the Spirit' – explorer, soldier and new age man. 'Blimpish colonialist who ended up a premature hippy', advocating unity of world religions and sexual liberation. Crossed the Gobi desert from Peking and climbed over the Mustagh Pass into India and so naturally, of course, was a player in the Great Game. In 1889 he explored the Karakoram and in the following year the Pamirs. He led the 'famous' Mission into Tibet in 1903. Which led to a bloody massacre. Gen. MacDonald, in his confidential dispatch to Curzon, estimated that 628 Tibetan soldiers were killed and 222 were wounded. Younghusband himself described it as 'nothing but pure butchery'. Saying that it had been 'a pure massacre – brought on by the childishness of the Tibetan general'. (The Tibetan general had neither wanted to fight nor surrender). And so the Roof of the World was entered into, with the aid of machine guns and shrapnel shells. Tibet occupied such a place in the British imagination, at the time, that John Buchan wrote, 'that it was impossible for the least sentimental to avoid a certain regret for the drawing back of the curtain'. But a Knighthood would be given to Col. Younghusband for pulling back the curtain. And Sir Francis would continue on his spiritual quest. Remaining convinced of the spiritual Power of mountains. 'That there is a power at work in the whole making for higher and forcing good out of evil is the secret of the Himalaya'. And he said that the climbing of Mount Everest 'would do a great deal of good. It would elevate the human spirit'.

Mallory wrote to Winthrop Young saying: 'The Everest expedition has become a sort of religious pilgrimage in his eyes. I expect I shall end by sitting at his feet, hearing tales of Lhasa and the Chitral'.

It was largely as a result of the 'success' of Younghusband's mission to Lhasa and the subsequent signing of a treaty between Britain and Tibet, that the Everest expeditions became possible in the 1920s. Prior to it, all foreigners had been denied access to Tibet.

For the exploration, the mission to Lhasa and the later exotic and florid growth of Younghusband's new age 'theoretical spirituality', the aliens on Altair and his Sacred Dramas – the whole fascinating and extraordinary story, couched in the form of a personal quest – *Younghusband – The Last Great Imperial Adventurer* by Patrick French (HarperCollins Publishers 1994.) For the Great Game and another account of Younghusband's role in it – *The Great Game* by Peter Hopkirk, O.U.P. 1990. Many readers will doubtless have fond memories still, of reading Rudyard Kipling's classic adventure story *Kim,* which romantically portrays the excitement of the Great Game *in the splendid days of Empire.*

Notes to Part XIV

The imagination sets the reach of vision in the mind. . . and as Einstein said, 'Imagination is more important than knowledge'. In a memorable summing up to his essay in *Voices from the Summit*, *Journey to a Calmer State of Mind*, Leo Houlding concluded by saying: 'Perception and vision are our keys to evolution in rock climbing'. As they are the key to everything really. Vision here, of course, functions as the more anodyne and acceptable word for imagination. Our society seemingly is not comfortable with the word. Hauntingly, imagination makes no entry in the *Oxford Companion to the Mind* ed. by Richard Gregory. In the words of the title of one of Samuel Beckett's short works: *Imagination Dead Imagine.*

Notes to Part XV

What shall I tell you?

What shall we tell you? Tales, marvellous tales
Of ships and stars and isles where good men rest,
Where nevermore the rose of sunset pales,
And winds and shadows fall towards the West.

From *The Golden Journey to Samarkand* by James Elroy Flecker. While teaching at Charterhouse, Mallory took the young Robert Graves under his wing and encouraged his interest in poetry. Among the modern poets he introduced him to was Flecker. The poem first appeared in his collection *The Golden Journey* (1922).

The poem was included as the final song in Flecker's exotic, 'Arabian' play *Hassan,* 'a poetic drama', which was given a sumptuous production by Basil Dean, with music by Frederick Delius at His Majesty's Theatre. 'A story of lovers who suffer death by torture rather than separation'. It was a big hit in the 1920s.

The crag's repeat. . . A naive clergyman, according to Matthew Arnold, once asked William Wordsworth, if he had written anything else, apart from his best-selling *Guide to the Lakes.*

O.G. (Owen Glynne) Jones (1867–99) One of the great pioneers of British rock-climbing. In 1896 he published *Rock Climbing in the English Lake District*, in which he laid out the first system of classification of difficulty. It contained thirty full-page reproductions of the Abraham brothers' photographs. It was an immediate success and became a classic. In his book *Camera on the Crags* Alan Hankinson describes it as, 'the definitive portrait of the spirit of the days when rock climbing was young'. He goes on to say that Jones 'was what the rock climbing world came to call, some fifty years later, 'a hard man', prepared to tackle new problems in all kinds of conditions, under ice or snow, through waterfalls, in blizzards or in gales'. And from one of George Abraham's books he quotes the following:

'The modern popularity of British rock climbing owes its inception either directly or indirectly to the life-work of Owen Glynne Jones. His favourite theory was that all men should climb, and they would be better for it this was in contradistinction to the somewhat dog-in-the-manger idea which then prevailed, that the joys of the mountains were only for men of liberal education and of the higher walks of life. Would that he could see the fruition of his wish!'

He was killed on the Dent Blanche, in August 1899, when his guide, Furrer, slipped and fell pulling Jones and a second guide, Vuignier with him to their deaths. Together with the Abraham brothers he had been excitedly planning an ambitious trip to Kangchenjunga. Walt Unsworth, in the *Encyclopaedia of Mountaineering,* at the end of the lengthy listing of his climbs says, 'this list is noteworthy in that many climbs are still among the most popular in Britain'. Which eloquently conveys the extent of his remarkable achievement.

Alan Hankinson's book *Camera on the Crags – a portfolio of early climbing photographs by the Abraham brothers* – Is a labour of love and fascinating for anyone interested in the early history of climbing and of photography. And it admirably demonstrates the dramatic power, the depth of grain and atmosphere of good black and white photography. These photographs really do stand the test of time. It is sadly out of print but was published by Heinemann in 1975.

Whymper, Edward (1840–1911) The greatest pioneer of the Golden Age of climbing and one of the first legends of mountaineering. A wood-engraver by profession, who's woodcuts Hilaire Belloc thought 'to be a high example of the national genius'. (High praise from Belloc who thought he was one himself). Whymper fell in love with the

Alps, while he was touring the region in order to make sketches for his work. Forever associated with the first ascent of the Matterhorn and the subsequent tragic accident that occurred on the descent. In the wake of which, the Press of Britain and the Continent united in denouncing mountaineering as an absurd and utterly unjustifiable sport. Queen Victoria inquired of her Ministers, whether it could not be stopped by law. The Golden Age was at an end. Of the tragic incident on the Matterhorn, Walt Unsworth says 'more has been written about the dramatic events of that day than any other event in mountaineering'.

Whymper wrote one of the classics of climbing literature, *Scrambles Amongst the Alps in the years 1860-9* – universally known as *Scrambles.* In it he provides his own account of what happened on the descent on that fateful day in July 1865. Mallory gave a copy of it to Ruth to read, shortly before their wedding, to aid in his wooing her round to the love of mountains.

As a result of his experiences in South America in 1891, which convinced him that there were errors in the readings of aneroid barometers, he published a pamphlet which also contained suggestions for improvements – *How to Use the Aneroid Barometer* – which Mallory refers to in part XXVII, while on the summit and befuddled by exhaustion and lack of oxygen. Muddling by free-association 'Chaucer's astrolabe', 'Whymper's aneroid' and his own altimeter, (Chaucer had written a treatise on the astrolabe).

The Whymper line – (by analogy to the Plimsoll line) The line that separates the difficult form the dangerous. Not to be confused with the fear barrier, which as Don Whillans memorably observed is 'bloody near the ground, because if I fell from there I'd damage meself'.

Ghost of a departed quantity . . . Bishop Berkeley's famous attack in 1734, *The Analyst* – a masterpiece of polemics – on the role of the vanishing increments (infinitesimals) that played so crucial a role in Newton's calculus. 'And what are these . . . vanishing increments? They are neither finite quantities, nor quantities infinitely small, nor yet nothing. May we not call them ghosts of departed quantities.'

Letters of John Keats. – Call the world if you please 'The vale of Soul-making'. From letters to George & Georgina Keats (14 February – 3 May 1819) pp. 249-50. Ed. by Robert Gittings (O.U.P., 1970)

Milton the Awakener – From Blake's extraordinary autobiographical poem *Milton,* that charts the journey of his own spiritual realisation and his prophetic education. In it Blake takes on the persona of the seventeenth century Christian poet John Milton (a Christian and a Republican – Blake was working on his poem at the time of the French Revolution, which Blake ardently supported). Readers will all be familiar with the prefatory poem to *Milton,* as the words, set to music by Sir Hubert Parry, have become universally known as the hymn *Jerusalem.* Because it has been taken completely out of context, as Patrick French says, in his biography of Younghusband (the man in 1916 responsible for it becoming the hymn that we all now know), '*Jerusalem's* popularity rests on the very instability of its symbolic value. Nobody is quite sure what it does represent'. He goes on dismissively to say that what Blake intended is now irrelevant. That is a view with which I don't concur.

Blake, in the persona of Milton, 'Milton the Awakener', confronts us through the spiritual journey that Milton undertakes in the poem to awaken to the false reality, the external reality created by our own selfhood. The world we perceive as being 'without', the world we externalise and desire and wish to control. And which in its turn controls us. Mallory, as all of us unrealised sentient beings, is caught up in the masquerade of the changeling nicknamed Free Will. Which in Buddhist terminology is known as the world of *samsara* (illusion – the world created by our ego-centred perception) and which Blake sees in exactly the same way, as being the false reality (illusion) created by our selfhood. Hence Blake's Milton announces, 'I in my Selfhood am that Satan' – being 'an incrustation over my immortal Spirit, a Selfhood which must be put off and annihilated alway'.

Through Milton, Blake the mystic urges each person to see himself or herself, 'like the diamond which tho' cloth'd/ In rugged covering in the mine, is open all within,/ And in his hallowed centre holds the heavens of bright eternity'.

All those who are familiar with the *Vajra* (Diamond) teachings of Buddhism will be immediately struck by the correspondence. Blake's visionary Milton announces his spiritual mission:

I come to discover before Heaven & Hell the Self righteousness
In all its Hypocritic turpitude, opening to every eye
These wonders of Satan's holiness ...

And in the prefatory poem *Milton* (Jerusalem), it is the feet of this prophetic Milton,

'Milton the Awakener' that Blake wonderingly questions the reality of having been 'in ancient time walking upon England's mountains green'. And then, making his own determined response to take up Milton's challenge in the poem, 'to go in fearless majesty annihilating Self', Blake calls forth:

Bring me my Bow of burning gold;
Bring me my Arrows of desire;

The desire is the mystics desire for the putting off of 'all that is not of god alone'. For the state of being at one with the immortal spirit, that which is eternal: in Buddhist terminology – the Buddha nature.

But all those who have or who are struggling with their own personal problems/ 'demons' or against some difficult grain in their egos, and even more so, those seeking to reach enlightenment, will understand the need now for the magical weapons, that Blake calls for in the poem. And the earnest nature of his vow, 'I will not cease from mental strife'. Neither self-mastery nor enlightenment come to us at all easily, to say the least. And Blake's Jerusalem, that he summons us to build, corresponds to the Buddhist Shambhala, where, in Blake's words, 'each shall mutually annihilate himself (i.e. his ego-centred self) for others' good'.

Blake would regard the current religious fundamentalism that plagues our own time as a manifestation of 'the Self righteousness in all its Hypocritic turpitude' and as exemplifying 'the wonders of Satan's holiness'.

Mallory's generation were the first to 'discover' William Blake, and one of Mallory's closest friends was Geoffrey Keynes, the man who compiled the first bibliography of all Blake's works. Keynes was at work on this project before 1914 and subsequently 'took up the threads', to use his phrase, in 1918. The bibliography was published by the Chiswick Press with the financial support of the Grolier Club of New York, in 1921. Both the Oxford and Cambridge University Presses had turned it down.

The Gates of Memory Geoffrey Keynes (O.U.P. pbk.ed. 1983)

Notes to Part XVI

Thou hast conquered, soulless industrialisation ... secularly parodies Swinburne's *Hymn to Proserpine*, which presents the cultivated but jaded pagan view of the establishment of Christianity and the death of the old gods:

Thou hast conquered, pale Gallilean; the world has grown
grey from thy breath ...

A poem which a man of Mallory's generation, with his interest in poetry, would have been familiar and with his modern literary taste, would have seen as rather 'old hat', hence the irreverent spoof and the secular parody of it. It was first published in the collection *Poems and ballads* (1866).

The Man with the Hoe – a reference to a painting by the French artist Jean–Francois Millet (1814 – 1875) that was first exhibited at the Salon in 1862. *The Man with a Hoe* quickly became one of the most controversial pictures in the later 1800s in France.

Millet himself wrote of its subject matter:

'Sometimes in places where the land is poor, you see figures hoeing and digging. From time to time one raises himself up and straightens his back . . . wiping his forehand with the back of his hand. "Thou shalt eat of thy bread in the seat of thy brow". Is this the gay, jovial work some people would have us believe in? But nevertheless, to me it is true humanity and great poetry.'

The painting inspired an American schoolteacher, Charles Edward Anson Markham (1852 – 1940) to write a poem in 1889 about it with the same title, which became as famous as the painting. The poem, as the painting, is a powerful indictment of the inhumanity of man to man – of the perniciousness of the subjugation and exploitation of other human beings.

Bowed by the weight of centuries he leans
Upon his hoe and gazes on the ground,
The emptiness of ages in his face,
And on his back, the burden of the world.
Who made him dead to rapture and despair,
A thing that grieves not and never hopes,
Stolid and stunned, a brother to the ox?
Who loosened and let down that brutal jaw?
Whose was the hand that slanted back the brow?
Whose brain blew out the light within his brain?

In November of 1916 Mallory had written that 'he had developed quite a special feeling for men digging; he would like to have been able to draw them, like Millet's figures, only '*more there*'. 'You would feel all the stiffness of the clay and the spiritual comfort of getting the better of it.'

Notes to Part XVII

Archer Thomson, James Merriman (1863-1912) – Regarded as the outstanding pioneer of Welsh rock-climbing. Co-author of the first Welsh climbers' guidebook *The Climb's on Lliwedd* (1909). There was a well-known jingle about it:

The climber goeth forth to climb on Lliwedd,
And seeketh him a way where man hath trod,
But which of all the thousand routes he doeth
Is known only to Andrews – and to Thomson.

Albeit not the most memorable of jingles, but it conveys something of the standing that the guide had in those years. Thomson discovered many of the Welsh cliffs: Idwal Slabs, Glyder Fawr, Craig yr Ysfa, Clogwyn y Person, Ysgolion Duon, Pillar of Elidyr. His climb of the Black Cleft of Dinas Mot was considered for some time the hardest climb in Wales. The Girdle Traverse that he made on Lliwedd in 1907, was a new invention at the time: which has, of course, since been followed on almost every cliff. Herford, Mallory & Young followed it on December 1914, before they dropped down to repeat the traverse along a new line.

Initially opposed to guide books, he was won round finally when he saw the guide-book compiled by the Abraham brothers. He did not, however, use a classification system. The climbs he did on Lliwedd were considered in their day as suitable only for the most advance experts. And Lliwedd was 'the Mecca of climbers' and the guidebook was the *vade mecum* of the climbers of Mallory's generation. I have quoted directly from *The Climbs on Lliwedd* in the climbing sections, as Mallory would have been so thoroughly conversant with it. The following extract of his description of the climb of the Far East Buttress contains almost all of the quotations and will convey something of his style. But those interested in speculating, as to whether or not Mallory climbed the second step, may find this passage of particular interest.

'It has been stated that good holds exist, but they are none the less undiscoverable when the hands are benumbed by icy water. Then, at any rate, it becomes necessary to improvise new tactics. The width of the chimney permits the climber to lie sideways at full length and to wedge in the forearm above his head. With this as a lever and anchor it is possible to writhe up one or two feet. Friction materially increased by inspiration, provides the mainstay, while the arm is moved up. The process is repeated until the third dimension of man precludes all possible further progress. One hand now grasps a yellow stone in the fissure; the right leg is brought out of the chimney, and thrust up to a sloping step on the face: a strenuous effort is then needed to overcome the combined forces of friction and gravity and escape from the vice. The spot thus reached is then hardly a landing-place – it accommodates one foot only, but the desired rest can be obtained by leaning back against a projection; in this half recumbent attitude above and athwart the crack we are in a good position to enjoy the circumambient air, a wide view of the face, and an unobstructed outlook over Cwm Dyli.'

Notes to Part XVIII

Moore & *Principia Ethica* – G.E. Moore (1873 – 1958) was, as many readers will probably know, one of the most influential British philosophers of the twentieth century. The *Principia* was published in 1903 and Lytton Strachey trumpeted, 'The age of reason has come'. Lowes Dickinson said that it 'made a kind of furore among my friends at Cambridge'. In the book Moore attacked cognitivist naturalism as mistaken in principle, for committing what he called the 'naturalistic fallacy'. Moore believed that he could show that ethical facts could not be natural facts and that therefore ethical knowledge would have to rest on non-sensory intuition. This, needless to say, was not what really captured the imagination at the time. It was Chapter VI, on The Ideal, where Moore famously concluded: 'By far the most valuable things, which we can imagine are certain states of consciousness, which may be roughly described as the pleasures of human intercourse and the enjoyment of beautiful objects'. In the Table of Contents, at the front, this was conveniently summarised, 'it is obvious that personal affection and aesthetic enjoyments include by far the greatest goods with which we are acquainted'. And the chapter – 'a scripture for youthful believers before the First World War'– became the 'manifesto' of the Bloomsbury Group.

Maynard Keynes thought that compared to it, 'the New Testament is a handbook for politicians'. And in his essay went on to say:

'it is better than Plato because it is quite free from fancy. It conveys the beauty of the literalness of Moore's mind, and the pure and passionate intensity of his vision, *unfanciful* and undressed-up. Moore had a nightmare once in which he could not distinguish propositions from tables. But even when he was awake, he could not distinguish love and beauty and truth from the furniture. They took on the same definition of outline, the same stable, solid, objective qualities of common–sense reality.'

Bertrand Russell in the preface to *Principles of Mathematics* (1903) said:
'On fundamental questions of philosophy, my position, in all chief features, is derived from G. E. Moore.'

Leonard Woolf, in his autobiography, vividly conveys the extent of Moore's influence over his generation and the Cambridge of the time. 'The colour of our minds and thought had been given to us by the climate of Cambridge and Moore's philosophy, much as the climate of England gives one colour to the face of an Englishman while the climate of India gives a different colour to a Tamil'.

Almost inevitably, the particular section that Mallory paraphrases comes from the chapter on The Ideal (p. 187); the passage beginning, 'And secondly there is the more subtle error which consists in neglecting the principle of organic unities'. 'The symphonic whole', in Mallory's own phrase.

In his autobiography, Moore with disarming frankness asserts, 'I do not think that the world or the sciences would ever have suggested to me any philosophical problems. What has suggested problems to me is things which other philosophers have said about the world or the sciences'. And as Hao Wang, in *From Mathematics to Philosophy* says, 'it is hard to resist the temptation to ask what would happen if all philosophers were like this'.

As Mallory would have been familiar with both Pater and Moore's work, it is interesting to compare the following from Pater's famous conclusion of his *Renaissance*:

'A counted number of pulses only is given to us of variegated, dramatic life. How may we see in them all that is to be seen in them by the finest senses? How shall we pass most swiftly from point to point, and be present always were the greatest number of vital forces unite in their purest energy?

To burn always with this hard bright, gem-like flame, to maintain this ecstasy, is success in life ... While all melts beneath our feet, we may well catch at any exquisite passion or any contribution to knowledge that seems by a lifted horizon to set the spirit free for a moment ...'

With Moore's: '*By far the most valuable things that we can imagine, are certain states of consciousness*' (my italics), which may be roughly described as the pleasures of human intercourse and the enjoyment of beautiful objects'. Pater has been rightly condemned for his solipsism and also for his 'philosophy of sensationalist hedonism' but are Moore's prized 'states of consciousness' any less solipsistic or his 'pleasures of human intercourse and the enjoyment of beautiful objects' any less hedonistic? Was the Cambridge of 1903 really so very far away from the Oxford of 1873?

Moore, G. E. *Principia Ethica* C.U.P. (pbk. rep. 1966). Russell, Bertrand. *Principles of Mathematics* C.U.P. (1903). Levy, Paul. *Moore – G. E. Moore and the Cambridge Apostles,* (O.U.P. 1981)

Notes to Part XXII

Guru Padmasambhava (lotus-born one) – known generally in Tibet as Guru Rimpoche (precious guru) was instrumental in establishing Buddhism in Tibet in the eighth century. The myth of his ascent of Everest on a sunbeam is probably a metaphoric tale conveying simply to the ordinary people his attainment of enlightenment (i.e. Buddhahood). In his book *Meeting the Buddhas* Vessantara provides a fascinating summary of an extraordinary biography about him called *The Life & Liberation of Padmasambhava* and of how he received enlightenment in a cemetery called Mysterious Paths of Beatitude. For those interested in finding out more about buddha-nature and the matrix-of-one-gone-thus – Mahamudra: The Quintessence of Mind and Meditation by Takpo Tashi Namgyal trans. by Lobsang P. Lhallungpa Motilal Banarsidas Delhi 1993. Written in the sixteenth century, it is regarded as one of the great Tibetan classics on meditation and methods for realising enlightenment.

The Mummery Crack – A drop of the man himself, on the final stage of the ascent of the summit of the Grépon – from *My Climbs in the Alps and Caucasus* (London, 1895).

'At one or two places progress was very difficult, the crack being in part too wide to afford any hold, and forcing the climber on to the face of the slab. I subsequently found that at the worst point my longer reach enabled me to get hold of a small protuberance with one finger, but how Venetz, whose reach is certainly a foot less than mine managed to get up has never satisfactorily been explained. At the next stage the crack narrows, and a stone has conveniently jammed itself exactly where it is wanted: beyond, the right-hand side of the crack gets broken, and it is a matter of comparative ease to pull oneself on to the top. This top then forms a narrow, but perfectly easy and level, path to the gully leading to the hole in the ridge. We found this hole or doorway guarded by a great splinter of rock, so loose that an unwary touch would probably have been resented with remorseless severity, and the impertinent traveller hurled on to the Nantillon glacier. Squeezing through, we stepped on to a little plateau covered with the debris of frost-riven rock.

Burgener then proposed, amid the reverent and appreciative silence of the company, that libations should be duly poured from a bottle of Bouvier. This religious ceremony having been fittingly observed (the Western form, I take it, of the prayers offered by pious Buddhists on reaching the crest of some Tibetan pass) we proceeded to attack a little cleft overhanging the Mer de Glâce, and cleverly protected at the top by a projecting rock. Above this we found ourselves in a sort of granite crevasse, and as this, so far as we could discover, had no bottom, we had to hotch ourselves along with our knees against one side, and our backs against the other. Burgener at this point exhibited most painful anxiety, and his 'Herr Gott! geben Sie Acht!" had the very ring of tears in its earnest entreaty. On my emergence into daylight his anxiety was explained. Was not the knapsack on my shoulders, and were not sundry half-bottles of Bouvier in the knapsack?'

An example of Alpine humour, that would not have met with Donald Robertson's approval. In the 1950s, Showell Styles took a more benign view of Mummery's style, seeing it as exhibiting 'the characteristic jocularities of the Victorians ... notably much simple fun and innuendo centring round the famous "bottle of Bouvier".' And welcomed the fact that, 'gone at last is all preoccupation with boiling-point thermometers, goitre, glacier mechanics or the past history of Alpine townships. Mummery climbed for the joy of the game alone'.

O for the wings of an Avro – Most readers will spot the reference to the song 'Oh for the wings of a dove' and many may still remember that Avro was once a famous name in aviation. Planes manufactured in the early days in Manchester by A.V. Roe & Co. (Perhaps mainly now in the renown of the Avro Lancaster bomber, of *Dam Busters* fame, the name of Avro lives on for posterity.)

- The issue of whether or not Mallory climbed the second rock step is possibly the most controversial and hotly debated. At the crux of the contention is whether or not he could have climbed the final headwall. Opinions vary considerably on this question. Initially, Conrad Anker, who solo climbed the headwall on the expedition in 1999, said that he thought Mallory could have done it, but shortly afterwards he changed his mind and has subsequently declared that Mallory could not have done it.

- In order to climb the headwall wall, it is necessary to make use of a vertically running crack, a strain slip cleavage that splits the rock face. The way that it is climbed requires the jamming in of the arm and the wedging in of the leg into the crack, in order for the climber to be able to lever himself up by means of the crack itself. As the crack is on the left side as you face the head wall, it is the left arm and leg that are required to act as the necessary levers.
- When Mallory's body was discovered, his watch was found inside his pocket. It was minus its crystal and also the minute hand was broken off and missing. Quite obviously it had been taken off and put there after it had been damaged. No traces of glass were found in his pocket. Mallory wore his watch on his left arm and facing inwards. The damage to the watch fits perfectly what would have happened, if he had forgotten to take it off and attempted an arm jamming and levering climb up a rock crack. Recently, I have read that the climber and writer, Jim Curran has also thought along this line. I would just like to go on to point out that there is absolutely no sign of any scratching or scoring on the watch face itself. This makes it therefore very difficult to account for the damage in any other way. A sufficiently hard knock necessary to either break or dislodge the crystal would surely have left some scoring or scratch marks on the watch face itself. Glass has a hardness of seven. And consider the fact that the watch has been carefully taken off and put away in his pocket. The watchstrap was thin and the buckle small, this was an operation requiring the removal of warm, outer gloves and the use of bare fingers. And it requires that at the time he did it, he was still in a sufficiently alert and well-functioning mental-state to care enough to be bothered to do this *and had the time*. And remember also that from 2pm that day until 4pm there was a snowstorm. I think the combination of the first consideration and the second fact enables us to say, with some degree of confidence, that he put the watch away, in his pocket for safekeeping, as stated in the text – at the lunchtime stop, shortly around or just after 1 pm. It would almost certainly have to have been done during the first half of the day. You wouldn't be fiddling about with your watch in a snowstorm and after 4pm, exhausted and with every minute of remaining daylight so vitally pre-

cious, it is hardly conceivable that Mallory then would be sufficiently concerned about his damaged watch, or have the time even to take it off and put it carefully in his pocket. This reinforces the argument in favour of the watch having been damaged whilst doing the crack climb of the Second Step. It fits in with the timing. And consider the difficulty of explaining how the crystal could have been knocked out, through all the protective padding of his outer glove and the sleeve of his tweed jacket *without leaving a single mark, dent or scratch on the face.*

- The headwall of the second rock step was first officially climbed by two, Chinese climbers in 1960, using combined tactics, 'Liu Lien-man offered Chu Yin-hua a leg up on to his shoulders'.
- Interestingly there are several accounts of Mallory using a 'human stepladder'; the technique of using the human ladder and the use of 'anatomical holds' had been well described and explained by Young in *Mountain Craft*. And Mallory, as we know, had reviewed the book and climbed a lot with Young, and its use seems to have been something of a showpiece for Mallory. This extract below, from David Robertson's biography, comes from an Austrian doctor and climber, Karl Blodig. Who, having been discountenanced by an ice chimney, thought along the following lines:

'I favoured going back and finding another route, but that did not please the second party at all. Mr Mallory climbed up, turned his back against the block of ice, wedged himself in the chimney as best he could, and brought Mr Reade up. Then Mr Mallory used him as a human stepladder and, with greatest dash and marvellous skill worked his way up the smooth surface until he disappeared from our view. Unanimous cries of 'Hurrah' hailed this extraordinary performance.'

- When Anker says that Mallory could not have climbed the Second Step, he is simply not comparing like with like. He climbed it solo, whereas it is highly unlikely, to say the very least, that Mallory would not have used combined tactics, using Sandy Irvine as a human ladder. Why should he have made things more difficult for himself?
- And of the two, Chinese climbers who did the climb in 1960, Walt Unsworth in his history of Everest says that, 'they were relatively inexperienced'. In 2003 Andy Politz, who had been on the Mallory & Irvine Research Expedition in 1999, came over to Britain and together with Duncan Lee followed three of Mallory's climbs. Of the final climb *Eastern Gutter* on the remote precipices of Llechog they said that 'not only was it a serious proposition with barely adequate protection, it was also a

contender for meeting the grade of HVS 5a (5.8)'. As a result of Mallory's laxness about recording his achievements, 'the details of the climb were lost for years, until 1980'. And as a result, the climb they say 'never became the test piece of it's day that it most certainly was'. Their conclusion, after repeating these three climbs, was that 'he was definitely an extremely talented and daring cragsman who was pushing the standards of the day'.

For Duncan Lee's article *George Mallory Master Craftsman?* – *High Magazine* Feb. 2003.

- The technical difficulty of the solo climb of the Second Step, has been assessed by Conrad Anker as 5.10 (British Grade E1). But remember he climbed it solo and did not use combined tactics. As did the two Chinese climbers 1963, who were, as stated above, 'relatively inexperienced'. So what would have stopped Mallory from doing exactly the same in 1924, using the combined tactics that were something of his speciality, of using the 'human stepladder' and achieving an equally successful result as the Chinese climbers. He was, after all, rather more than just a 'relatively inexperienced climber'.
- But pronouncements that he couldn't have done it, based on its technical grade as a solo climb, miss the mark. That E1 is not the measure of the reality of the climb done by the Chinese climbers, who used combined tactics, otherwise how could relatively inexperienced climbers have done it. These are quite simply two different orders of reality and each with a very different measure of technical grade of difficulty.

Note to part XXIV

- All versions of the events of the attempt on the summit that day, must take into consideration the fact of Irvine's ice axe, found in 1933 by Wyn Harris below the first rock step. Reportedly lying on 'boiler plate slabs'. 250 yards before that obstacle. And now also the fact that in 1999 the Mallory & Irvine Research Expedition retrieved an oxygen cylinder, No.9, which had been wedged into some rocks not far below the first rock step. Cylinder No.9 was found 620ft (190m) from the base of the first rock step. So 620 feet from 750 feet (250 yards) = 120feet. Allowing for the usual imprecision involved in judging distance and bearing in mind that Wyn Harris's figure is only a rough estimate after all. Then the distance between the axe and the cylinder may very well have been considerably less, in fact, than 150 feet. But given the relatively close proximity of the spent cylinder and the axe, I have connected these two facts and put them together in the narrative.

- The region where Irvine's ice axe was found sounds exactly like the place, that would have afforded a good view of all three rock steps and the summit beyond, with Mallory climbing up ahead in the foreground. In other words, making the perfect composition for a photograph. The Kodak Vestpocket Camera requires that a small bellows be pulled out, it is a delicate operation that would have required the putting down of the axe, as well as the removal of at least one of his outer gloves. This would explain the fact that the axe would appear to have been put down rather than dropped. Perhaps because that was, in fact, just how it was in actuality. And if then, as Mallory narrates, he had seen Mallory in difficulties with his oxygen set, then it becomes understandable how the ice axe could have been completely forgotten in the heat of the moment. This, at least, constructs a coherent, internally consistent narrative that fits the facts. It also provides a credible and reasonable explanation as to how Irvine might have left his axe behind. And one that does not make him out to be simply careless and incompetent. However, of course, simply because it is plausible and convincing is in itself no absolute guarantee of its truth.

Ghosts of Everest, Jochen Hemmleb, Larry A. Johnson & Eric R. Simonson (Macmillan 1999). Everest, Walt Unsworth (Grafton Books 1991)

Notes to part XXVI

Barnes the final stretch – refers, as many British readers will recognise, to the annual Oxford and Cambridge University Boat Race, a race rowed by two crews of eight over a 6.8km course on the Thames River. True to the British spirit of not regarding the vagaries of weather too seriously, it duly takes place in March. The race starts at Putney Bridge and the final stretch begins at Barnes Bridge, when the rowers have to dig deep into all their remaining reserves for the final sprint to the finishing line at Mortlake, just below Chiswick Bridge.

Sandy Irvine had begun rowing at Shrewsbury school where he became Captain of Boats. On his arrival at Merton College Oxford, he was shortly after offered a place in the Oxford Crew. And he was a proud member of the winning Oxford crew in 1923 and would definitely have been selected for the Oxford crew in 1924. He was consequently mortified by the news of Oxford's crushing defeat in 1924. The opportunity to go on the Everest expedition had, of course, taken priority. Julie Summers has written an excellent and affectionate biography of him, *Fearless on Everest: the Quest for Sandy Irvine* (Weidenfeld & Nicholson 2000). Her book also provides a good account of the extent of the modifications that Sandy Irvine undertook to the original gas apparatus, complete with photographs of the original sketches he made in his notebook, in order to develop the Mark V. oxygen set.

Mallory also, of course, was an oarsman and rowed for Magdalene College, Cambridge and was in 1907 Captain of the College Boat Club.

- We know, from Noel Odell's account, that at 4pm the wind dropped and the sun came out – the weather conditions on the mountain were perfect – and if Mallory & Irvine were approaching the summit, then they would have had the most seductive vision of 'the glittering prize', in Peter Boardman's memorable phrase. In the text I suggest that this is exactly what happened.

Notes to part XXVII

- It is necessary for any account of the events of that day to put forward an explanation as to how the crystal came to be missing from Mallory's altimeter – well, the account here provides one such attempt. It is at least within the required constraints of a consistent and complete narrative.
- The Everest researcher, Audrey Salkeld has quite rightly drawn attention to the fact that it is not entirely known for certain, whether Mallory had a photograph with him of his wife at the time. However, when Mallory's body was discovered, the inner wallet that he had hung round his neck, underneath his clothing, in which he cached his private correspondence contained no letters from his wife. Although there was a letter from his brother, his sister, a letter from someone he scarcely knew (Stella) and even a bill from Gamages: but no letters from his wife Ruth. Whatever doubt there may or may not be about Mallory having a photograph of his wife with him on the day, it is inconceivable that he did not have any letters from his wife with him. The problem facing those who do not believe that Mallory reached the summit is to provide a credible explanation for the absence of those letters.

Notes to Part XXVIII

Avalokiteshvara – In May 1911 Mallory went with his friend Cottie Saunders to see the exhibition of Chinese paintings at the British Museum. These had recently been bought and brought back by the explorer Aurel Stein, from the Caves of the 1,000 Buddhas at Tun-Huang. Both were particularly struck by a picture of the great *Earthly Paradise,* a painting of the paradise of Avalokiteshvara. Readers familiar with Buddhism will know, and as Vessantara in *Meeting the Buddhas* says, 'Avalokiteshvara could be described as the quintessential Bodhisattva, for he is the Bodhisattva of Compassion, and compassion is the distinguishing mark of the Bodhisattva.'. Devotion to Avalokiteshvara reached its height in Tibet, where he is known as Chenrezi.

The approximate phonetic English spelling of the name in Mallory's time, was Chongraysay: the name, of course, of the High Lama at the East Rongbuk Monastery. Chenrezi is regarded as the patron and guardian of the whole of Tibet. And the Dalai Lamas are considered to be manifestations of Avalokiteshvara. The High Lama of the East Rongbuk Monastery was also believed to be a manifestation of the Bodhisattva of Compassion. *Om mani padme hum* – is the mantra of Avalokiteshvara.

Robertson, David George *George Mallory.* London, 1969. Vessantara *Meeting the Buddhas: A Guide to Buddhas, Bodhisattvas and Tantric Deities.* Windhorse Publications, 1993

(Some of the frescoes from the walls of the Caves of the 1,000 Buddhas can be seen on the internet at www.chinapage.com/dunhuang)

Notes to Part XXXI

Pindar – (518-438 B.C.) Possibly the greatest Greek lyric poet – the Greeks compared him with an eagle – known for his Epinician Odes – choral songs written to celebrate and honour the victors in the great Games at Olympia, Delphi, Nemea and Corinth – the Odes cover the whole spectrum of Greek society – from politics and earthly competition, the weave of fate, through and into the rich mythology that informed the Ancient Greek world. 'Good fortune is the best and first of prizes'.

Notes to part XXXII

The Angel of Mons & the Comrade in White – most readers will probably know now that the former had its origins in a story written in 1914 by Arthur Machen, that appeared in a London evening paper. Machen's claim to originating it was hotly contested at the time. No less than eight books had appeared on the subject by 1918. All strongly contra Machen's claim, one bore the title *On the Side of the Angels* and there was even an Angel of Mons Waltz written by Walter Paree.

The Comrade in White is another battlefield myth: 'This mysterious one, whom the French called the Comrade in White, seemed to be everywhere at once. At Nancy, in Argonne, at Soissons and Ypres, everywhere men were talking of him with hushed voices'. This was written by an anonymous English soldier and appeared in *Life and Work* magazine in 1915.

For a fascinating compilation and account of all this folklore and legend from the First World War – James Hayward *Myths & Legends of the First World War*, Sutton Publishing, 2002.

The Charge of the Light Brigade – As most readers will know, a famous military blunder in the Crimean War – a splendid cavalry charge straight at the Russian artillery – and duly honoured and celebrated by the poet laureate at the time, Alfred Tennyson (1809–92) – in a thumping, Victorian 'cannons to right of them, cannons to left of them' rollicking poem. And anyone of Mallory's generation would have known the poem very well, and probably would have had to learn it by heart at school. In a letter to J. P. Farrar on the 2nd of July 1921, Mallory wrote, 'this (Rongbuk) glacier runs itself up into a cwm, like the Charge of the Light Brigade'. A great number of readers will doubtless recognise the parody of Tennyson's poem *The Charge of the Light Brigade* – 'Half a league, half a league, half a league onward etc.' in Mallory's 'Half a metre, half a metre, half a metre onward etc.'.

(Capt. Percy Farrrar was a member of the Everest Committee, a former President of the Alpine Club and described by Walt Unsworth as one of the greatest living Alpinists at the time.)

Notes to Part XXIX

How beautiful on the mountain . . . Isaiah I11. 7.

Almer – when Mallory was still at school at Winchester, an Ice Club was formed under the aegis of a schoolmaster, Graham Irving, who was keen to take young 'recruits' on climbing trips to the Alps. All the young members took to calling themselves by the names of the great Alpine guides. Mallory was Almer, after Christian Almer of Grindelwald, whose epitaph described him as '*Der besten Führer einer*'.

Notes to Part XXXII

Collie's spooky tale . . . Prof. John Norman Collie (1859 – 1942) described by Walt Unsworth as 'one of the greatest mountaineers of the turn of the century'. He was a member of the joint Royal Geographical Society & Alpine Club Everest Committee. Prof. Collie started what was to become the legend of the Big Grey Man – the 'Ferla Mor'– of Ben MacDhui. The story first broke in New Zealand, where Collie had been speaking to friends on a visit. Collie's story was sensationally reported by the local New Zealand papers, under the headline 'A Professor's Panic' and news of this reached Dr. A. M Kellas. Who duly wrote back to Collie, claiming that he had actually seen the Grey Man. Dr. Kellas was, as some readers may recall, the expedition doctor who died on the 1921 Everest Reconnaissance Expedition. For the whole story of the Big Grey Man, the lore and legend and the facts – *The Big Grey Man of Ben MacDhui* by Affleck Gray (Birlinn, 1994).

Dr. A. M. Kellas was the leading authority on the physiological effects of altitude and it is from his paper that Mallory quotes in part XXV. In 1914 Dr. Kellas had gone to Kamet, in the Kumaun Himalaya, where he scientifically studied the effects of high altitude on the human body. At the time of the Everest Reconnaissance Expedition he was fifty-three. Mallory wrote of him: 'Kellas I love already. He is beyond description Scotch and uncouth – altogether uncouth' and that he would 'form an admirable model to the stage for a farcical representation of an alchemist'. Concluding this description of him to his wife he said, 'he is an absolutely devoted and disinterested person'. It was Dr. Kellas, climbing on his expeditions in the Himalaya solely with local porters, who made the discovery 'that the best came from a remote valley in Nepal. They were called Sherpas'.

peaks, passes and glaciers – as many readers will recognise is a reference to the original papers read by the founding members of the Alpine Club, that were collected into the classic volume *Peaks, Passes and Glaciers* – 'a gospel of adventure' – the further papers subsequently became the *Alpine Journal.*

NoaNoa – Title of the Tahiti Journal of Paul Gauguin published in 1921

A chota peg of mummia. . . . As those of old drank mummia,
To fire their limbs of lead . . .
Mummia, Rupert Brooke

Mummia being an occult elixir containing, amongst other gruesome ingredients, ancient Egyptian mummies ground into fine powder (in Brooke's poem referred to as 'spiced imperial dust') reputedly either miraculously rejuvenating or possibly even imparting immortal life to those who drank it. Chota peg (*Anglo-Ind.*) a small drink (i.e a small measure of spirits) it was traditionally a whisky and soda: the mainstay of the British Raj.

'Mummery's Blood' – the recipe for . . . 'melt a sufficiency of snow', well, that's how 'the real men' did it, or first try it in the comfort of home. Heat the required amount of water in a pan over a stove (boil if supply is dodgy and allow to cool a little . . . you don't want to waste any of the alcohol). Add Bovril and rum to taste and stir well. The original recipe calls for equal parts of rum & Bovril. Which I have always understood as meaning that you make the Bovril first and then add an equal or should I say, complementary amount of rum accordingly. This is certainly highly effective. But, of course, it is necessary to experiment with this yourself. Those in search of the authentic experience will want to use Woods 100% proof Navy Rum . . . proceed with care. Serve while hot.

- Of all Mallory's injuries, one of the most painfully unpleasant sights, is that of his broken right ankle almost at right angles to his leg. It is an injury that seems difficult to account for as a result of a fall. Bodies are floppy in free-fall. His left foot that has obviously been caught in the rocks has had the boot wrenched of it and his remaining sock trails down after. It is exactly what you would expect to see resulting from such a fall. His foot being caught up and snagged in the rocks. But compare that injury now to the right ankle by contrast, the degree of it. And the fact that he still has his foot neatly in his climbing boot. I am neither a pathologist nor a forensic scientist but that injury strikes me as being inconsistent with a body in free-fall falling down a mountainside. No other injuries are apparent to his right leg, which you would reasonably expect to see if he had fallen on it in such a way as to break his ankle like that. And in free-fall his leg would have simply crumpled up under him, not offering the necessary resistance to sustain such an injury. And if it had wouldn't there be, of necessity further damage to the leg, certainly to the knee. It is an anomaly. In the narrative I have put forward the idea that, as Mallory was the lead climber and would therefore have been the last man coming down on the descent. And necessarily would therefore have been moving towards the right while descending, so that his right leg consequently would have been the one bearing most of his weight. That on hearing Irvine fall, he stood in to take the strain on the rope, straightening up on his right leg. Probably with only a narrow foothold that prevented him from being able to place his left foot down securely. Thus taking the full strain and weight of Irvine's falling body on his right leg. And Mallory had an old injury from the past, a fractured right ankle, and in prolonged exposure to the cold, old injuries start to 'play up'.

- In 1909 Mallory fell while climbing a sandstone outcrop and severely damaged his right ankle. Although not diagnosed at the time, he had in fact fractured it. The fracture subsequently healed badly. In 1917 it became so bad, that an Army doctor concluded that if he was to be of any further use to the British army, he would need an operation. Having barely recovered from that operation on his ankle he then crushed his right foot in a motor cycle accident. He spent a month in hospital as a result. And it was a further month again before he could walk in comfort.
- I suggest that, as a result of standing in to take the strain on the rope, Mallory's ankle, weakened from those injuries in the past, broke under the impact of the full weight of Irvine's falling body coming on the rope and consequently his leg gave way beneath him.

Notes to Part XXXVIII

Altum silentium – profound silence, in a literal sense the highest silence. The English word altitude being derived from Latin *altus – altum.* And straightforward Latin that has found it's way 'neat' into Chambers Dictionary.

Ah, God to see the branches stir ... And the later quote: *To smell the thrilling-sweet and rotten ...* come from Rupert Brooke's perhaps most well known poem *The Old Vicarage, Grantchester.*

- It is the weight of cumulative evidence, the damaged watch put away in his pocket, the missing letters from his wife, and the absence of 'pocket tiffin'; only a raisin or sticky bit of Kendal mint cake (depending on the account) and his small tin of beef lozenges (pemmican) were found on his body. And with the snow-goggles carefully and neatly put away in his pocket. The lack of remaining food supplies is significant, because it is an indicator that he had been up on the mountain for some considerable time. A fact reinforced by the snow-goggles found neatly put away in his pocket. This strongly points to his having been benighted. And that is eloquent of them having really achieved something. How long would they have spent struggling in the couloir during a snowstorm?
- But as some people suggest, he could have put his snow-goggles away at the start of the snowstorm, only this does not accord with the absence of pocket provisions, or the position of the body. Again if we take into consideration the weather conditions on that day. A snowstorm from 2pm to 4pm (Mallory and Irvine may possibly have been above it, if they had climbed the Second Step, but we cannot say for sure) but if Mallory did put the goggles away in his pocket during the snowstorm, then that requires that he fell sometime before 4pm. After which, as Odell reports, the mountain was bathed in sunshine. And if that was the case, how is it that he has managed to eat almost all of his supply of pocket tiffin? It more or less requires that he ate the lot at lunch! Not a bar of chocolate or Kendal mint cake or even an Agen prune was found. And you really wouldn't be doing much eating during a snowstorm. And how would you account for the missing letters from his wife? This scenario faces an even greater problem in accounting for the position where the body was found. From the injuries he sustained it is clear that he did not fall from the ridge. Why was he so low down in the rocks and not on the ridge if they had never been on for the summit. What have they been doing? If they didn't climb the Second Step and chose to follow Norton and Somervell's route and traverse round into the couloir, knowing that it was choked with loose unconsolidated snow, how long would they have remained there in a snowstorm? They would have had to have given up very quickly, and turned round in quick time, in order for them to get back to a position in line with where Mallory's body was eventually found. In order to be there before 4pm, when the sun came out.

After which Mallory would have needed to be wearing his snow-goggles until dusk. And this version of events also has to be squared, as stated, with Mallory having eaten his way through his pocket tiffin. Which leaves the further outstanding question, why in this case, would they have descended so far down from the ridge? They were in the rocks when the fall occurred. (Mallory's body is not sufficiently damaged for a fall from the ridge, other bodies lying in the area, that have fallen from the ridge are all severely mangled). And then, of course there is still the absence of his wife's letters to explain. And if he did not do any actual rock climbing, how did he manage to knock the crystal out of his watch, without leaving a scratch or mark on the face?

- There is one final outstanding detail – the missing crystal from Mallory's altimeter. If he hadn't done something remarkable that day, why has he had to use the altimeter? Having said that he wasn't interested in making any height records, and if he hadn't got any higher than Norton, who had not been using oxygen, would Mallory, so tired and gutted with all that disappointment, have really bothered to find out the exact height at which he turned back. Well, it is possible. And for those who believe he fell before 4pm (in keeping with their explanation of the pocketed snow-goggles) he would have to have done this in a snowstorm. So accounting for the damaged altimeter raises a further consideration.
- In the narrative I may have taken the 'artistic licence' of having Mallory make the summit attempt, using only two cylinders of oxygen (as he had stated that he would) in reality it is possible that he went on three. We know from the results of the arithmetic tests, conducted by Dr. Hingston, that Mallory was the least affected by altitude. He would have prospected the route on the previous afternoon and from the notes on the back of an envelope found on his body, it is clear that he was doing some serious calculations. But the issue, as to whether he went on two or three oxygen cylinders, is now probably undecidable; the reader must make his or her own judgement upon this matter.
- One caveat needs to be borne in mind, which I have not seen made in any of the suggested scenarios put forward to fill-in the detail of what may have happened on the climb that I have read. Something that was illustrated memorably for me, when I heard an American thriller writer, (Tom Clancy?) being interviewed shortly after 9. 11. He said that in his books he could easily get readers to believe the high-jacking of one plane for a suicide mission *but not four*. This demarcates the difference clearly between reality and fiction (credible fiction), in that the former is not

attendant upon our willing suspension of disbelief and the latter depends on it entirely. For a sense of how extraordinary the events could have been, the account provided in Walt Unsworth's book *Everest* of Peter Habeler's amazing descent, having made the first ascent without oxygen with Reinhold Messner, is surely one of the most powerfully evocative. 'Habeler confessed that he was scarcely conscious of his actions during the descent – it was as if he was an observer, watching somebody else climb'. I have borne this in mind, as far as possible, for the account given of Mallory's descent in the text. However, being fiction I could obviously not avail myself of Habeler's miraculous avalanche. He, after all, was only up against reality, not the reader's willing suspension of disbelief.

- The problem is to construct a complete, internally consistent, coherent narrative, which also accords with and respects all the facts that we have at present. In the narrative I have endeavoured to do that.

Mallory has taken on an almost mythic status in our time – become a legend – and inevitably there are those who make him out to be an heroic figure of almost incomparable stature and those who, understandably in reaction to that, feel the need to debunk the man. I think for most people, not caught up in this polarised debate – betwixt the reverential monument builders & the debunking demolition squad – it is obvious that between these two extremes lies the truth – the human reality. I have tried, within the constraints and limits of the work, to do justice to that human reality – rich, complex and fascinating, flawed and paradoxical, as it is our lot to be.

Acknowledgement: I would like to thank the Alpine Club for all the assistance that I received in doing the research for this book. Without the resource of the Alpine Club Library, with its unique and remarkable collection, this book could never have been written.

Glossary

In the text I have used a number of words that some readers may not be familiar with, therefore the provision of a helpful glossary seemed a useful idea. In trying to avoid the tired, descriptive adjectives, the deadened clichés and all that conspires with a dull, prosaic language of the common place, I have found it necessary, given the demands of the setting and the order of the undertaking, to use a rather more extended and poetic vocabulary and style than is usually the norm. As Wittgenstein says in the *Tractatus-Logico-Philosophicus*: 'The limits of my language mean the limits of my world'. Sometimes it is necessary to push at those limits.

All entries below from *The Shorter Oxford Dictionary* 1973 (with corrections 1978) unless otherwise stated.

Afterclap – An unexpected stroke after the recipient has ceased to be on his guard; a surprise happening after an affair is supposed to be at an end. I intend both senses of the word in the title.

Amphibological – Ambiguous.

Arefaction – Drying. Chambers Dictionary

Astrolabe – A medieval scientific instrument to take altitudes, and solve other problems in astronomy.

Aureate – Golden, gold coloured.

Azoic – Having no trace of life. Chambers Dictionary

Cantillation – Chanting.

Charivari – Cacophonous mock serenade, a cacophony of sound, din.

Crystallogenesis – The natural formation of crystals.

Crystallomancy – Divination by means of crystals – i.e. the snow crystals in Everest's snow plume divine the direction of the high altitude wind.

Declivitous – Having a considerable declivity, steep

Disadorned – To deprive of adornment.

Effulgence – Splendid radiance

Eldritch – Weird, eerie, uncanny: A Scottish word and one that Prof, Norman Collie who started the story of the Big Grey Man of Ben MacDhui and Dr. Kellas (also a Scot), who claimed to have seen it, would very likely have used in their own descriptions.

Empyrean – The highest and purest region of heaven: anciently, the sphere of pure fire, the highest heaven where the pure element of fire was supposed to subsist; in Christian use the abode of God and the angels.

Epitonic – Overstrained.

Exiguity – Scantiness. Chambers. And an Archer Thomson word

Glozing – Flattery. Glozing is *a tad archaic* but alliterates with glazing and seems to deserve a better fate than its current neglect and disuse. Mallory enjoyed words – 'orosophy' (see below) to give but one example.

Haecceity– The quality implied in the use of *this*, as this man; 'thisness', 'hereness and nowness'; individuality. The term derives from the Scholastic Philosopher, Dun Scotus, who had an enormous influence on the poet Gerard Manley Hopkins, who derived the inspiration for his words inscape and instressing from reading Dun Scotus

Heimweh – homesickness.

Hyaline – A) Transparent as glass, crystalline, vitreous: Chiefly *techn* B) 'A sea of glass like unto crystal' (Rev. 4:6) hence poetical for the smooth sea, the clear sky, or anything transparent. I do not see that there is here any conflict between the technical or poetical sense.

Illapse – n a sliding in – vi to glide in. Chambers. In the text I wanted that combined association and onomatopoeia of ill & lapse on the ear, to convey the pejorative sense of sliding into the mechanical way of doing things, the *illapse* into the unthinking nature of it.

Implex – involved, complicated (Latin *implexus,* from *in* into and plectere to twine) So involved, complicated *and intertwined* as indeed the cognitive architecture and 'operating systems' that embed and maintain our sense of self must be intricately intertwined.

Inenarrable – That cannot be narrated, told, or described: unspeakable. The S.O.D. provides the example from Chapman (1716) 'Earth's inenarrable continent'. A word Mallory's friend, the poet Rupert Brooke, had used in one of the best of his later poems *The Great Lover* (1914) and that Mallory would have known.

Inscape – Coined by the poet Gerard Manley Hopkins – the essential inner nature or distinctive form of a person. Chambers Dictionary. By analogy and contrast to land-scape, to denote the inner 'landscape' of the mind: the modern coinage now being mindscape but Mallory would most certainly would have known Hopkins's term inscape.

Insouciance – indifferent, unconcerned, apathetic.

Instress – The force of energy which sustains an inscape, the sensation of inscape. Coined by Gerard Manley Hopkins Chambers Dictionary.

Lucent – Shining, bright, luminous.

Moliminous – A great effort, *esp.* any physical effort made by the body in carrying out a natural function. This definition comes from Chambers Dictionary 1993. The Shorter Oxford Dictionary has 'Molimen *Pl.* molimina 1865 . . . ending in the strained, lexicog-rapher's pedantry, 'the straining to bring about the catamenia': this entry does not look as if it has been revised since 1865.

Oneiric– belonging to dreams. Chambers Dictionary. The Shorter Oxford (2 Vols.) straddles it from oneirocritic, oneirology to oneiroscopist but does not contain an entry for oneiric.

Orisons – Prayers

Orogeny & orogenic – from orogenesis mountain building; the process that takes place during an orogeny – orogenic belt region of the earth's crust that has been subjected to an orogeny.

Orosophy – As far as I can tell Mallory's own coinage. From orology the scientific study of mountains. The oro coming from the Greek word for mountain and instead of the suffix *logy* (*logos* discourse) he has put *sophy*; from the Greek *sophia* wisdom: so literally mountain wisdom.

Pandect – A treatise covering the whole of any subject. Chambers Dictionary

Petrographic province – (*geol)* A region characterised by a group of genetically related rocks. Chambers Dictionary. And a region not charted in The Shorter Oxford Dictionary.

Piltdown man – a once supposed very early man represented by parts of a skull found at *Piltdown* Sussex (1912), the skull was exposed as a fake in 1953. Chambers Dictionary. The Piltdown man did not make it into the S. O.D.

Prelapsarian – Belonging or relating to the Fall: in Judaeo-Christian belief the first man & woman, Adam & Eve sinned (fell from innocence & grace) and were cast out of Eden (paradise) by their wrathful creator & god Yahweh/Yehovah) In other words, since the very beginning– primordially. In the interest of greater clarity I have taken the liberty of elaborating upon the very basic entry in Chambers Dictionary. (The S.O.D. contains no entry).

Pyrrhic – a victory gained at too great a cost.

Revenant – person who returns from along absence *esp*. from the dead; ghost.

Ruderal – Growing in wasteland. Chambers Dictionary

Salade – (medieval armour) a light helmet extending over the back of the neck (just in fact as a pith helmet does)

Scandent – Climbing. Chambers Dictionary (not in the S.O.D.)

Scapulimancy – Divination by means of the cracks in a shoulder blade. Chambers Dictionary.

Scintillant – Sparkling. Chambers Dictionary

Scrannel – Thin, meagre. Now chiefly after Milton: Harsh, unmelodious.

Sinistral – Situated on the left-hand side also has the meaning: likely or designed to cause mischief.

Snout-faced basinet – M.E. Steel helmet with a pointed visor that resembled a pig's face. *A Dictionary of Chivalry* Grant Uden (Longmans 1968) Both S.O.D. & Chambers provide short entry for basinet, but nothing more.

Stultiloquence – foolish or senseless talk, twaddle. In this instance the 'senseless talk' of forced, inconsequential, polite conversation.

Supernal – Existing or dwelling in the heavens, exalted, situated in or belonging to the sky, celestial, heavenly: supremely great, excellent or 'divine'. Used here in as many of the above senses as the reader can have comfortably resonating in mind.

Tabernacle – (Lit. a tent) Of men as spiritual beings dwelling in the temporary 'fleshy tabernacle' (tent) of the body. Mallory's father was a vicar and consequently this biblical language would have been deeply ingrained in him.

Theophany – a manifestation or appearance of deity to man. Chambers Dictionary
Transilluminate – to throw a strong light through.

Turpitude – Baseness, depravity , vileness.

Whelming – Overturning, overthrowing, submerging, overpowering. Chambers Dictionary